LOST CHILD

A compelling novel of love, heartbreak and family

GRETTA MULROONEY

JOFFE
BOOKS

Published 2016 by Joffe Books, London.

www.joffebooks.com

ISBN- 978-1-911021-42-1

In memory of my parents,
Hugh and Peggy

PROLOGUE

The girl woke, feeling empty. This happened often, waking hungry in the early hours. She had a storybook about a boy being taken to a night kitchen where bread was made for the morning and her mother laughed at her trips for biscuits, saying that she was Elva in the night kitchen. The Mickey Mouse clock by her bed said 2.20. She lay for a few minutes, watching the luminous silver stars and pale crescent moons on her bedroom ceiling, listening to the clumping footsteps in the flat above. *Riff-raff,* her mother called the people upstairs, a word that she loved to repeat; said fast, it sounded like a dog's bark. She thought about the ginger biscuits in the kitchen, home-made by her mother, who bought real ginger on the market to grate into the dough. Her mother's arm flashed up and down as she worked so that when Elva squeezed her eyes closed, it became a blur. She imagined the spice of the dark, crumbly biscuits on her tongue, delaying the moment when she would get up and eat some, her mouth watering. Someone overhead flushed a toilet and that made her want to go, so she slid out of bed and went to the bathroom. The plastic seat was pleasantly cool against her warm skin; this summer was so hot, they were sleeping with just thin sheets on their beds.

Her mother was asleep on the sofa as she passed through the living-room on her way to the kitchen. The biscuit tin had dark yellow flowers on it and there was a trick to opening it because the lid was wonky. She banged the lid once, glancing at her mother, half expecting her to start and stretch, then sit up and look for her soft pumps, saying that she hadn't meant to doze off. But her mother slept on and she quickly pulled the lid off and took two biscuits. She stood and watched her mother as she ate, the moist dough sticking to her tongue, and washed the biscuits down with a glass of milk. The cold coated her mouth and calmed the fieriness of the ginger.

She rinsed her glass and put it upside down on the draining board, then moved to her mother and shook her shoulder because she got a frozen neck when she fell asleep on the sofa. She'd ask Elva to rub it for her, very hard, dig her bony fingers in. When she didn't move Elva shook her again, then again, calling her name. She was floppy and her eyes stayed closed. Her long hair trailed across the cushion. Elva thought she must be ill. Maybe she had sleeping sickness, Elva had read about that in the encyclopaedia. She leaned down by her mother's face and smelled a trace of garlic from the spaghetti Bolognese they'd had for supper. Garlic warded off evil spirits, her mother told her.

She knew about 999 and she dialled and said that her mum was sick, speaking the address slowly although her heart was racing. While she was waiting for the ambulance, she fetched the temperature strip from the drawer and put it on her mother's forehead. That was the first thing her mother did when Elva said she didn't feel well. It would change colour, blue to green to orange, depending on how high her temperature was. Her mother called it *the temperature rainbow*. Elva pressed it to her skin but nothing happened, no rainbow colours appeared. She kept it there, just in case, until the ambulance men knocked on the door, but it stayed dark, no colours blooming, the blues and greens and oranges of a life.

She stood by the sofa in her nightdress while the ambulance men bent over her mother.

'What's your mum's name, sweetheart?' one of them asked and when she told him he said: 'Suzy, Suzy, can you hear me?'

Then there was a long silence broken by music suddenly erupting from above, the deep thud of bass guitars. This was when she would hear her mother knock on the ceiling with the kitchen mop and call, *turn that damned racket off, there are people trying to sleep down here!* But her mother was having no trouble sleeping; the noise didn't bother her at all tonight. The tall ambulance man with glasses, the one who'd called her sweetheart, said to her that she should put some clothes on because they were going to have to take her mum to hospital. He asked if her mum had any tablets and she said only herbal ones.

'Has she got sleeping sickness?' she asked and he glanced at his companion and said: 'we'll get her to hospital, then we'll know more, sweetheart. Is your dad around, or an aunty or granny?' She told him that she didn't know her dad and added what her mother had always said, that she and Elva were each other's family, they had only each other in the whole wide world. The tall man patted her shoulder and went to the phone.

In her room she pulled on shorts and a T-shirt and neatened her bed, smoothing the sheet. When they came back from the hospital, her mother would be pleased to see her room looking ship-shape. She heard the door of the flat opening and when she went back to the living-room her mother was being carried out on a stretcher, a blanket over her. Elva thought that she would get too warm, wrapped up like that. During the hot days her mother threw open the windows, saying, *give me air, I must have air.*

3

A small, balding man had arrived. He pushed the door to and wiped his brow. 'Hallo' he said, 'my name's Gary. I'm very sorry to have to tell you this, Elva, but your mum's died. We don't know why yet, they'll find that out at the hospital. I'm going to take you to be looked after while your mum's with the doctors.'

She stared at him, wondering how he knew her name. The music blared from above, *thudthudthud*. The man's forehead was wet.

'They're riff-raff up there,' she told him and he nodded but she could tell he didn't understand. Then she said, 'will I die of it too, what my mum got?' but she spoke so hesitantly that the man didn't hear over the drowning music. He was looking around the sparsely furnished flat, thinking that this skinny girl called Elva might never recover from what had happened in this place on this night. He looked down at her small, anxious face, saw the worried frown that would probably cloud her adult features. Chances of happiness, he thought, few.

CHAPTER 1

Hearts can be broken quickly or slowly, over time. I've had friends whose hearts have been gradually splintered, eroded so that the final break is a hushed anguish. Nathan's heart and mine were broken sharply, at one blow and we turned on each other, separated in our grief.

I sit on the rocks, gazing at the sea, thinking that I should go back and prepare breakfast. I don't move. I am held by the pale sun and the solitude. The September sea is restless today, grey-green, the waves murmuring. It's a day for pacing. Spray blows into my face, the salt scratching at my skin. The sky is vast and bleached, the sun high but faint. I had never been to Norfolk before Nathan brought me. When I exclaimed at the expanse of sky he said that he only fully understood what a prison London was when he came here.

That was the day he lay stretched on the sand, arms above his head, his body a long line and said: 'This is it, I have you and Matt and I want for nothing else.'

This has been nothing like last summer, the season that I will always think of as the summer of fire, when our lives were consumed. There has been little sun and the breeze blowing from the sea is contrary, changing direction, whipping up the sand. Some people despair of it, shaking their heads. I am glad of it, glad of the cooler temperatures and the evening chill and because it keeps the tourists away. It is easier to think when the sky is not a furnace.

I finger the beads in my jeans pocket. My grandfather gave me the mother of pearl rosary when I left Dublin to make a life with Nathan. He must have known that I was a feeble Catholic by then but I've been glad of its comfort. It was the rosary that I turned to afterwards in the autumn, solacing myself and praying for Nathan, for all of us as I walked alone through olive groves, fingering the smooth beads. At night I lay with the rosary laced between my fingers. When I woke suddenly before dawn, jolted by a nightmare, reaching for Nathan and finding emptiness, I pressed the cross hard into my palm.

'Are you sure he's the one for you, pet?' my grandfather asked the day I told him I was getting married. 'Absolutely, he's the one. We're meant to be,' I replied, love making me so certain. Then, it seemed to me that Nathan and I were in a magic circle, untouchable. Our ordinary lives had been transformed by something like grace, that intangible blessing bestowed by faith. I forgot that ordinary lives can also be transformed by naivety, misfortune, and accident, that once you are in a state of grace, you can fall from it.

I didn't care where I went last autumn. I ended up on a Greek island because it was the first flight available on that evening after I pleaded with Nathan and he replied in a remote, high voice: 'nothing you say can make any difference to me.' I felt like a wanderer in my own life. I wrote to Nathan care of Connie. On the veranda of a small guesthouse I used a leaking biro on thin blue airmail paper:

> *I can't say anything to help, I know that. It's terrible to love you and yet not be able to help you. I can hardly help myself. I have always believed that love can heal and yet now I find that all my long-held beliefs are ashes. You loved my optimism, but I think*

*that it had never truly been put to the test; I was just
lucky enough never to have walked on the shadowed
side of the street. Affection and love aren't enough and
especially if they're not yours to give. They weren't
enough for Elva; how can temporary love ever be
enough? I see that now. We were all perhaps foolish,
unthinking, but I was the catalyst and that weighs
heavy on me.*

*I love you so much. You are all I hoped for, all I
wanted, all I want.*

I walked along the cicada-thronged road to post my
letter. I was wearing the sarong that Connie had made. It
was creased and smelled faintly of marijuana but I hadn't
washed it because the soft cloth held mine and Nathan's
breath and sweat. I fingered the envelope, wondering that
a small, fragile square of paper could hold such feverish,
anguished words; there should at least be singe marks at
the edges.

There is a boat beached down on the rim of the sea.
Matt played in it last summer, pretending to be a pirate. I
bought him an eye-patch from a joke shop and a garish felt
parrot for his shoulder. Nathan would pick out the tune of
Captain Pugwash on a cheap harmonica from the pound
shop in Hunstanton. I lay back on the shale, watching
them, digging my toes into the heap of sand that Jess and
Elva had left when they shaped a huge fort. The boat is
holed and uncared for, the wood rotting, another year's
tide and salt damage.

I walk down to the shore, my sandals puffing the sand.
Matt scoured this beach for shells to give his mother,
filling his bucket, taking them down to the water. He
washed them all meticulously, a labour of love, the hem of
his smart French shorts dipping in the rock pools. I climb
into the boat and sit on the seat, which just holds under
my weight. There is the sharp smell of salt water, the smell
of love making.

I rock the boat to soothe myself. There are small items of debris drifting in on the tide. I scoop up a shred of seaweed and a crab shell and cradle them in my cupped palms.

I think of Nathan sleeping, his mouth compressed, his hand gripping the pillow. I will leave him for a while longer, safe in the medicated slumber his doctor dispenses in foil packs.

Flotsam and jetsam: that was how Gary referred to Elva. It applied to us all afterwards.

I am a salvager now. That is my job in this chiller summer. I am a salvager of wrecked lives and I must move carefully, cautiously, reclaiming what I can.

* * *

We met at a party at my cousin Cormac's house in Dublin. I nearly hadn't gone, thinking of the lesson plans and marking I had to do but I'd roused myself; it was Saturday, I was entitled to a break. There was a brisk wind blowing in from the sea at Dalkey and I bent my head, feeling it whip my hair. Autumn was my season; I always had a surge of energy when the leaves started to turn.

The party was a crowded, smoky affair, full of Cormac's business friends and people he'd been at Trinity with. Cormac's circle were generally hearty types, men who liked practical jokes and women who played sports. He and they were riding high on the booming economy; they talked of shares and global markets. Someone had bought a racehorse and Cormac was doing a deal on being a partner in a leisure centre. I blinked through cigarette fug as he introduced me to a man with thick chestnut hair, the colour of polished conkers.

'This is May; this is Nathan, one of my compadres. He studied much harder than me at Trinity; he can interpret in six languages.'

'Which ones?'

'Spanish, German, French, Japanese, Italian and Mandarin,' Nathan said.

'And he has a smattering of the Gaelic, of course,' Cormac added.

'Oh yes, that too,' Nathan smiled. He looked exhausted, his creased blue eyes heavy. He was one of those tall men who automatically stoop when speaking. I noticed his mouth, his shapely, symmetrical lips. I've always believed that features reflect character and I surmised that he might be contained, centred. I also surmised that he might be one of the many compadres that Cormac slept with.

'I warn you,' Cormac told Nathan, waving to a newcomer, 'May's my favourite cousin, so look after her. She's the conscience of the family, the only one of us doing anything really worthwhile.'

'And what would that be?' Nathan asked.

'I suppose he means that I teach children with learning problems. I don't think it's more worthwhile than other jobs.' I looked away, concerned that he might find me self-important. People were frequently over impressed when they discovered that I taught, even if it was children who my grandmother insisted on calling 'sub-normal'.

We talked and he yawned, apologizing; he'd just come back from conferences in Riga and Tokyo, stopping off in Dublin for Cormac's birthday. He travelled a lot, he explained, the company he worked for in London provided a service for businesses all over the globe.

'I've not slept properly for over a week,' he groaned, his voice scratchy. 'Sometimes I feel as if I leave bits of myself all around the world, you know, mislay pieces — like luggage that gets lost on airport conveyor belts.'

'Or like a trail in the sky, part of the white vapour we see when we look up.' I liked that idea, that some of a traveller's atoms would disperse amongst the clouds as he flew back and forth over continents, ploughing the heavens.

He smiled. 'Something like that. Then there's the waking up in the morning and not being able to remember where I am.'

'We all do that,' I said, 'but usually after a skinful.'

He made a shape with his hand around my head. 'Your hair looks as if it's been spun.'

'It was the wind,' I said, 'that easterly wind off the sea. My mother would say I look like the wreck of the Hesperus.'

He was tapping with his fingers on the side of his glass. I listened for a moment.

'"Paper Moon",' I said.

He nodded. He tapped again.

'"Eleanor Rigby". You made it harder.'

'Of course, I'd hardly make it simpler.' He looked into his glass, then at me. 'Are you married?' he asked.

'No.'

'Ever been married?'

'No. You?'

'Yes, and divorced. I've a three-year-old son who lives with me in London.'

'Oh; I thought you might be gay, as you know Cormac.'

'Well I could be, even so, I suppose, but I'm not. So that sorts out that agenda. Unless you are?'

'No.'

He pinched the bridge of his nose with his long fingers and I startled myself by imagining his touch on my skin. The window behind me was open, letting in the tangy October evening. A chill snaked along the back of my neck but I was glad of it because the house was too warm, thick with the heat of bodies and shouted conversation. There were a few fallen, yellowing leaves stuck to the glass, I could see them from the corner of my eye. I could smell a bonfire, even though I knew that there wasn't one lit and I realized that my senses were playing tricks, summoning memories of other seasons. I tilted my head, believing that the room was holding its breath. There was an oval mirror on the wall opposite and when I glanced in it and saw our reflected image, our other selves, it was as if I had lived this moment before.

'I play the saxophone,' he was saying. 'I'm playing next weekend in London. Will you come over and listen?'

'I will, yes.' I liked the way he came to the point, his directness.

He nodded. 'That's good, good.' He drained his drink, throwing his head back. 'I'm done in,' he said, 'you're the only thing keeping me on my feet.'

I looked at him, the fading light falling on his face and the wine glass and cocktail olive in my hands seemed things of beauty.

* * *

I said that I would marry Nathan the night I heard him play for the first time, in a smoky basement off Frith Street. There was a stillness about him that invaded my thoughts; in repose, he could look almost severe. When he did his solos he closed his eyes, leaning into his instrument, his shoulders concentrated, as if this was when his energy was released. The sight of him moved me, my breathing tightened. I knew in that moment that I loved him and I thought that if I never felt this again, it would last me until my sight failed and my bones grew brittle. He played *April in Paris, Take Five, Fly Me To The Moon* and *She Moved through the Fair*. I listened to the rich tone, the notes that caught like gasps, seeming to echo my own yearning. Watching him, I knew that he had gone into a world of his own, somewhere where he was unreachable and I both envied and admired his withdrawal. I talked to people, trying to hear and be heard above the music and conversation. There were a couple who were teachers like myself and I discussed the differences between the Irish and English education systems; I didn't say so, but it seemed to me that the Irish valued education more. Looking up from refreshing my wine, I saw that Nathan had returned from wherever he had been and was watching me. I raised my glass to him, aware of his focus.

It was a mild night and we walked back from the tube through the dark streets to his flat, saying little, our steps rhyming. He carried his saxophone, swinging the black case. I was conscious of a shift in the world, as if a veil had been pulled back, as if I had never been quite conscious of my own feet on the ground before. He took my hand and tucked it in his pocket. It seemed to me then that love was simple and fluid, like the stream that flowed by my grandfather's house.

His garden flat was untidy, strewn with toys and plates with toast crusts on. It smelled of herbs and a fruit I couldn't pinpoint. Later, I discovered that it was pomegranate, which his son Matt devoured, spooning the tiny seeds as he roamed the rooms. I banged my ankle on a bicycle in the hallway and he bent to look at it, putting one hand firmly on the bone. His touch was sure, almost impersonal.

'No damage done,' he said, looking up at me with his weary jet lag eyes.

In his bedroom he kissed my neck. 'You look like the Spanish lady, with your long dress and your black hair and your combs,' he told me. 'As in the song. You know the song?'

'I do, my grandmother used to sing it:

As I went down to Dublin city
At the hour of twelve at night
Who should I see but the Spanish lady
Combing her hair in the pale moonlight
First she washed it, then she dried it
Over a fire of amber coal
In all my life I ne'er did see
A maid so sweet about the soul.

My mother claims that one of those Spanish sailors from the Armada got friendly with my Connemara ancestors, hence the hair and brown eyes.'

'Eyes like wood smoke,' he said, 'that misty smoke that turf produces.' He picked up a soapstone figure of an elephant, ran his fingers across its smooth back. 'I'm eight years older than you; my job takes me away regularly. I smoke marijuana when I'm not working, probably too much, my only excuse being that it helps me sleep and it got me through the last couple of years and my divorce; living with Matt is like having a guerrilla fighter around. I'm not looking for a substitute mother for Matt, it's important that you understand that. That's it, that's all.'

I kissed his hands and the hollow of his throat and drew him down beside me. We lay, reading each other's faces and when we made love, he looked into my eyes, held my gaze and I thought that he was the first man who had ever done that, the first man who hadn't found passion somehow embarrassing.

In the early hours he caught my hand, opened his eyes and sat up to light a joint, plumping his pillows. I took a pull when he passed it to me, although I didn't much care for the bitter taste.

He told me then about his ex-wife, Veronica, his voice cracked and tired in the dark. She was a flight attendant; they'd met on a trip to Sydney. She'd handed him his Pernod, they'd chatted briefly, then during the night at length, whispered while the other passengers slept. A year later they married. Two years later, Veronica had propped a note by the kettle to say that she was leaving him for Michel, a French pilot she'd fallen for in Dubai. She'd doubled back after heading for Heathrow one morning, packed her things and vanished. He collected Matt from nursery and came home to a ransacked flat; at first he thought there had been a burglary. There had, in a way: a burglary of his trust, his life. His bed was wide and deep with a beech headboard, a relic from his marriage and we lay close in the middle of it. Veronica was in Paris now, with Michel. Matt stayed with Nathan, and Veronica didn't object. Once a month she flew to London and took Matt back for a week. She never explained to Nathan how she could leave her son. He said that he believed that she let him keep Matt through guilt. For months, he agonized over what it was that he did or failed to do that caused her to leave him.

'Maybe,' I said, 'there was nothing you could have done. Maybe it was just chance, just bad luck that she met someone else at that time. Events sometimes overtake people.'

He took a deep draw on his joint. 'I don't know. My aunt used to say, "If I didn't have bad luck, I'd have no luck at all." Mind you, she was one of life's pessimists; every cloud had a lead lining. When I got accepted for university she sent me a card saying, "if it was raining soup, you'd have a spoon".'

'The opposite of that is, "If it was raining soup, you'd have a fork." Or, as Cormac says, "If there was only a rasher of bacon to eat, I'd be Jewish".'

He pulled me close, holding my head between his hands. The skin on his palms was curiously rough and wrinkled. 'Tell me what you know,' he said, teasingly.

I stretched my fingers against his chest. 'I know that the world's my oyster and that an elephant never forgets and . . . I know that there's a man in the moon who eats the green cheese.'

As dawn broke in a lemon haze, revealing his face on the pillow, he said, 'I have to tell you, I'm afraid, that an elephant has no memory at all.' He stroked my hair back. 'You'll be my girl, then, you'll be my love.'

I agreed.

* * *

Matt was a generous boy with a trusting nature. He accepted my arrival in his life with equanimity. He was robust, with sturdy limbs, fair hair and Nathan's tender, washed-blue eyes. His energy was boundless. He was picking up French on his stays in Paris and would lapse into a form of Franglais when he was cross: *'Du pain,* Daddy, I want *du pain!'*

'May's a funny name,' he said the day Nathan introduced me.

'I'm called May because I was born in May,' I told him.

'Then There's May blossom, Our Lady of the May, Maypole, Mayfair, May queen, nuts in May and may I have this dance,' Nathan said, picking Matt up and whirling him through the air.

'Maymaymaymaymaymay,' Matt chanted, delirious with pleasure, hiccupping.

We picked him up from nursery on that first day. When he saw Nathan he raced to the gate, his legs pumping. He sat on his father's shoulders, pulling his ears, demanding samosas for tea. He had learned to count to twenty in both English and French and repeated the numbers over and over, until Nathan told him to put a sock in it, which caused him great amusement. We stopped at an Indian take-away for the samosas. While we waited for them we tried morsels of the sweets set out for tasting on the counter. I preferred the coconut wedge, Nathan the milky slice flavoured with cardamom. Unusually for a child, Matt didn't ask for sweets. Nathan told me that this might be because Veronica never allowed him to have them and I thought how odd it must be to have a part-time parent who pulled strings from afar.

We ate the samosas with chutney and yoghurt in front of the television while Matt watched cartoons. My tongue still held a trace of coconut and this added to the strangeness of sitting at five o'clock in the day with the curtains half drawn against the sun, watching Spiderman and crunching spices. It was like an afternoon visit to the cinema, which always seemed an illicit pleasure. I licked my fingers and drew air into my mouth to cool me down.

Matt turned time around and there were traces of him everywhere, like a remorseless tide: toys, vests and T-shirts, battered books, pictures of blobs executed in watercolours, bits of crisps, half-eaten apples. He smelled of cinnamon, his favourite topping on toast. When he was tired, he became pale and irritable. He tolerated me then, but it was Nathan he wanted, Nathan he cried for.

I stayed for weekends and during half-terms. We established a haphazard routine, punctuated by my returns to Dublin and Nathan's work schedules, which involved several weeks away followed by a period at home. Occasionally, I found something of Veronica's still in the flat: a pair of tights stuffed at the back of the airing cupboard; a silk scarf in a kitchen drawer; a frayed swimming costume at the bottom of the laundry basket, *long body, high leg*. I held them in my hands, absorbing their texture. The scarf smelled of a musky scent. I had a sudden feeling of vulnerability, as if I was an intruder, then I threw them away without mentioning them.

Matt had two photographs of his mother by his bed; she was tall, with short blonde hair and a direct gaze. In one, she held him on her jutting hip, laughing at the camera. In the other, she was in smart uniform, standing in the doorway of a plane and holding a tray. It struck me that Veronica and I were physical opposites. Matt had her wide mouth and hair and referred to her as *ma belle maman*.

* * *

We agreed to marry in early April. I resigned from my job and packed my possessions. Cormac took me for a drink on the night before I left Dublin. He looked at my trunk and suitcases stacked in the living-room of my flat and nodded.

'Time to move on,' he said. In the bar, he toasted my future. For once, his gaze wasn't constantly flitting, taking in any promising talent. 'I think you're brave, by the way,' he told me.

'Brave? Why?'

'Taking on a man with a kid. Taking on Veronica.'

I didn't understand, of course. Then, I thought that marriages ended with divorce. I knew no better, didn't have any friends who were divorced, wasn't aware of the tightly knotted skeins that can still bind.

'I'm not "taking on" Veronica,' I said lightly, sipping my wine, 'I think Michel's done that.'

Cormac looked shrewd. 'It's a jigsaw and you're another piece fitting in, let's say. She might not like you, might have a different picture of Nathan and Matt in her mind's eye. You can still be possessive about what you've thrown away.'

This hadn't struck me. I'd envisaged a civilized exchange of courtesies between two sets of lives.

'I suppose that's possible, but it's not as if we're going to have to see much of each other, I'm sure we can manage the situation. Nathan often takes Matt to the airport to meet her when she's having him for the week and once he's old enough to fly unaccompanied, she won't even have to travel over.'

Cormac smiled. 'I meant more that she might not like the *fact* of you: a usurper. Another woman tucking her child in at night.'

I frowned at him. It wasn't the farewell I'd been anticipating; evenings with Cormac were occasions of laughter and gossip, details of his multi-faceted love-life. The bar suddenly seemed too noisy.

'She left Nathan, after all,' I said. 'She must have realized he'd meet someone else. I don't see that she has any reason to resent his new partner.' She's happy, I was thinking, why wouldn't she want Nathan to be?

'Ah, logical May, rational May. If only people were always rational. If only I knew why I don't fancy the guy over there who's giving me the eye.' He lit a cigarette. The smoke mingled with his aromatic aftershave.

'Stop being such a Cassandra,' I said, annoyed. 'I thought you brought me for a drink to wish me well.'

He apologized, said he was just an old moany queen and I should ignore him.

'You know some of us gay men, always looking for the drama in a situation,' he added, ordering us another carafe of wine, launching into a story about a Brazilian he'd met at the theatre.

CHAPTER 2

We had a small, quiet wedding. My parents, who had emigrated to New Zealand while I was at university, sent us a cheque and a crate of champagne. Nathan's sister Connie organized the reception we requested, a picnic in her huge back garden. The day started warm and grew warmer, licked by the promised heat to come. I was glad that I had bought a sleeveless dress. Matt had a few sips of champagne and entertained us with his giggles. Nathan swept him up, tickled him under the ear, then cupped the back of my head in his free hand and told me that I was now his kith and kin.

At the end of April we moved into a house in Muswell Hill, not far from Connie and her family. As we drove there, heat shimmered around the car and across the bonnet, searing the air. The forecast was for an intense summer; drought was already predicted. When we drew up outside the house the roses in the front garden had come into full dusky pink blossom. Matt ran to them as soon as he had been released from the back seat and reached for a flower, shaking it hard. Nathan swept him up under one arm and gave him the key to open the door. I stood back, looking up at the house, anticipating the life we would have, the love we would make, the children we would create. I cupped the buds of a rose, pressing my fingers into its soft petals, the blooms forming a scented veil around my head.

That afternoon, when Matt was having a nap, Nathan uncorked the last bottle of my parents' champagne and we sat out on the patio with our glasses. There was crazy paving and a couple of white enamel sinks, the deep kind once used in sculleries, with bright red geraniums growing in them. The geraniums flared back at the sun, as if daring it to grow hotter. Colours were sharp and clear, the clematis by the fence a vibrant purple. When I placed my hand on my lap, the cotton weave of my sundress felt dense and textured. The afternoon sun glinted on Nathan's curly hair, striking copper sparks.

The patio was already littered with Matt's toys and his vast, round yellow paddling pool. Nathan looked up at the sun, then took a handkerchief from his pocket and made a hat for me, saying that I mustn't get burned. When he fitted it on my head his palm brushed my cheek and I felt as if his touch, not the sun, might burn me.

I gestured at the overgrown plot of grass and earth at the bottom of the garden. 'I've got plans for there. I'm going to grow things. I'm going to dig and grow lettuce and beans and peas, carrots and little crunchy green peppers and maybe courgettes.' I could see it all, lush rows of fresh, juicy produce; we would be able to wander out and pick our meals as the mood seized us.

'Do you know about gardening?'

'Not a lot, but I watched my father and I used to help - or maybe hinder him. I'm sure it's all gone in by osmosis. I've always known that I'd grow things one day, when I had a house and a garden.'

'Putting all kinds of roots down.'

'Exactly.'

'Can we have tomatoes too, those cherry ones?'

'We can. We can have whatever we like.'

When we'd finished the champagne we sat in the paddling pool, stirring the tepid water with our arms. Nathan had to put his feet over the sides. There was grit in the bottom of the pool, bits of leaves and yellow Lego and a crust of Matt's blackened lunchtime toast; he liked it almost burned. The crimson flowers on my dress looked as if they were floating in the water. I'd had only one glass of champagne but I felt tipsy. I kicked my toes and stretched them against the pattern of blue ducks on the rim of the pool. Nathan caught my hands in his and pulled me against him, in between his legs, making a rowing motion. He had rowed at university and the muscles in his arms and thighs were still solid; when I pressed my fingers into them, they stayed rigid. He said he'd have to be careful and exercise, or they'd run to fat. Backwards and forwards, backwards and forwards he shifted; I watched his rippling shadow in the water. He liked to let his hair grow when he had time off and with his bushy curls and broad shoulders, he might have been Neptune sitting behind me in our own small sea. He sang:

> *Row, row, row your boat*
> *Gently down the stream,*
> *Merrily, merrily, merrily, merrily;*
> *Life is but a dream.*

'You know,' I said, looking up at him, narrowing my eyes against the sun, 'you look a bit like George Bernard Shaw.'

He applauded. 'Now, that's very perceptive of you. He's a distant relative, old George, on my great grandmother's side. She was a Gurly, which was his mother's name. I hope you're impressed.'

'I am,' I said truthfully.

'There's no need to be. As GBS said of his family, "drink and lunacy are minor specialities." My grandmother had enough electric shock treatment to deplete the national grid and the year before she died she believed that the neighbours were urinating into her teabags.'

I was taken aback but I laughed with him. 'Did any of your family ever meet GBS?'

'No, he avoided his relatives and there had been some ancient disagreement, the kind that families are so skilled at. I was hoping to have a calmer, more reflective life than many of my forebears but I seem to have already managed a few hitches.' He was silent for a moment, running his hands in the water. 'I suppose,' he said, slowly, tentatively, 'that you were hoping to meet someone uncomplicated, not a divorced man with a young child in tow.'

I laid my head back against his chest. 'I think I was hoping to find you, although I didn't know it.'

He bent down and kissed the top of my head, saying my name, and I closed my eyes; it felt like a blessing.

'I'm glad Matt's got this week to settle in, before he goes to Paris,' he said lazily.

Veronica had phoned the previous evening to confirm flight times. Whenever I answered, she didn't acknowledge me in any way, but asked crisply for Nathan. I might have been a secretary. When I mentioned this to Nathan, saying that I found it petty, he laughed, said that that was just her way, she'd never been much good on the phone.

'Did Veronica say anything about our wedding?'

'Not really.'

'When will I meet her?'

'In good time. Let's settle first, there's no rush. I think she has to be in London for a couple of days sometime this summer. Her mother lives in Richmond. Now, we were gliding down a winding stream, weren't we?'

I sang with him:

> *Merrily, merrily, merrily, merrily, merrily, Life is but a dream.*

He caught my hand and held it to his face. His cheek was rough; he needed to shave twice a day. When we first met I had complained about the rash his stubble left on my skin. He placed his mouth close to my ear, whispering, 'tell me what you know today.'

I turned, pretending a serious concentration. 'I know that infinity plus infinity equals infinity, that the sheer willpower of the passengers keeps a plane in the sky and that there's no lead in a lead pencil.' I yawned, limbs lazy with heat and love. 'There'll never be another summer like this,' I said.

Afterwards, fingering my grandfather's rosary, I could only pray that my words would prove true.

* * *

I set off for an interview at Cedar End children's home towards the beginning of June. That had been the plan we made; we'd get settled in the house, then I'd apply for a job. I rubbed my hands together to calm my nerves. This was only my second job interview in teaching and I was conscious of being in a strange city. The advertisement for the post at Cedar End — a teacher cum care worker — stated, 'we need a special person to help make our children feel special.' That appealed to me and when I showed it to Nathan he said he was sure I'd fit the bill. He was packing for ten days in Moscow and Berlin and I watched the way he methodically folded his white cotton shirts and suits, moving between wardrobe and case; his deft, sure movements could make me feel weak. When he wore his smart business clothes he seemed to move away from me; he was different, apart, a player in a world I knew little of. When he came home, I could never relax until he took them off.

The heat outside was a shock. The streets burned, the baking air trapped between the buildings. I drove slowly to Cedar End, sniffing fumes and the sudden, pungent scent of drains, the sun striking my arm through the open window. I was still noticing the small differences between Dublin and London; here, the houses in Estate Agent windows had prices on, there were dozens of Indian restaurants, charity shops abounded and when a funeral passed by no one stopped as a mark of respect. A sallow-faced woman holding a bunch of heather stepped out in front of the car at a traffic light.

'Lucky heather, love, lucky heather, go on, buy some for luck, so you will.' The woman's teeth were blackened and full of gaps. I gave her fifty pence and bought some because the woman was an Irish tinker. I might even have encountered her before, on O'Connell Bridge.

I was feeling a little dazed by the heat and I shook my head, pressing my ears and swallowing. My palms were slippery with sweat. My A-Z slid around on the front seat and I put a hand out, tucking it back. I liked to read the names of London streets, my lips moving, tasting them. 'Limehouse Causeway, Hans Street, Beauvoir Town, Black Horse Road, Homerton High Street, Bartholomew Villas, Crooked Billet,' I murmured, a city litany. I knew Dublin like the back of my hand but there were thousands of roads, crescents and lanes in the A-Z that I was unaware of, that I could never know. I thought of the people living in those grids who I was yet to meet, heard them say, 'I can't believe you've not been here long, you know London better than I do!' Nathan had told me of a man he met who thought that Primrose Hill was a person.

I searched the glove compartment for a pack of skin wipes and ran them over my neck, arms and hands. They smelled of lemon balm, soothing. I was pleasantly surprised when I turned the corner of Cedar Road that day. I'd been envisaging the home as an old-fashioned Victorian place, possibly gloomy, something Dickensian. Cedar End was a wide, sixties-built three- storey building with huge picture windows and a large, turfed back garden. Inside, the building was warm and bright. My footsteps rang on varnished pine flooring. It was just after lunch and the air smelled of beef stew and bleach.

Ms Cartwright, my interviewer, was in her fifties, a harassed looking woman with elegant legs. She was soft-spoken, her fine grey hair caught up in a tidy French pleat. She smelled of an old-fashioned scent, something with hyacinths in. The breeze from the slightly opened window behind her ruffled a few stray hairs on her neck. She seemed rather genteel for someone who worked for local government, with her single string of pearls and delicate hands but I found her reassuring; Ms Cartwright bolstered my idea that this was a job where I could make a real contribution.

'Why a job in London rather than Ireland?' Ms Cartwright asked.

'I've just got married and moved here; my husband's based in London.' *Husband* was still strange and formal on my tongue; it seemed to refer to a person other than Nathan.

'And why did you decide on special education when you graduated?'

'I like the idea of teaching small groups or individuals, the focus of that and of knowing that I can make a difference to children who are troubled.'

Ms Cartwright nodded and made a note. 'If I could speak to a good friend of yours, what would they say about you?' she asked.

I was thrown for a moment, then recovered. 'Well, I think they'd say I'm an optimist and I have a respect for other people's dignity. They'd tell you I can be a bit forgetful and that I love music and literature.' I paused. 'I hope they'd say that I believe in humanity, its frailty and power.'

Ms Cartwright underlined something, then put her notepad down. She stressed that the troubled children who came to Cedar End might have been abused, neglected, suffered poverty, have experienced family tribulations or simply been abandoned. They needed love, kindness and understanding; she leaned forwards and cupped her hands as if to demonstrate a wealth of empathy. I saw no problems there; 'that love is all there is, is all we know of love,' I quoted, telling Ms Cartwright that the lines were from a poem by Emily Dickinson.

'We'd ask you to do a night duty, sleeping in once a week. Would that be a problem for you?'

'No. My sister-in-law lives near and she looks after my stepson when we're at work. He often stays the night with her, there's no difficulty there.'

The interview lasted just thirty minutes. Ms Cartwright escorted me to the door, straightening a tangled curtain on the way and bade me a warm farewell, saying that she would let me know as soon as possible about the post.

Later that night, when Nathan called from a hotel in Moscow, I told him that I'd been offered and accepted the job.

'The woman who interviewed me said that the children would have suffered *tribulations*,' I told him. 'Isn't that a wonderful word?'

I heard my own voice echo and his return, distorted.

'It is,' he said, 'it's biblical. Is Matt asleep?'

'Yes. He had four stories. He's restless; it's so hot.'

'Poor you. I have air-conditioning, the only advantage of being here.'

When we'd finished talking I went into the garden and lay on top of a sleeping bag. We had taken to sleeping out there on some nights, glad of the light breeze that came after midnight, the door propped open so that we'd hear Matt if he woke. In the thick dark we would make love quietly, skin gluing. Nathan would reach a hand out and pick a leaf of the lemon geranium, running it on my neck and shoulders. I was still unused to his departures and returns, the disjointment to our lives. Earlier, Matt had cried for him, becoming enraged. 'I want Daddy!' he had howled, refusing to be calmed until he was allowed to wear one of his father's immaculate shirts. He had it on in bed, rucked up around his waist. I tracked a plane across the sky and allowed the hum of London to crowd into my mind, to stop me missing Nathan.

* * *

The sun beat hard against the kitchen window. It illuminated the dust where Matt had drawn a face with protruding teeth. The purple pendants of a wisteria framed the top of the glass, like a painted frieze. There was the whine of a vacuum cleaner from next door. I wondered that anyone would want to do such housework in the morning heat. When it was Nathan's turn to vacuum he did it late at night, when it was cooler, when Matt had gone to bed. He stripped off and cleaned naked, the light shining on his long, muscled thighs; I would idle on the sofa, watching him, marvelling at the curve of his back, lifting my feet when instructed. Sometimes I'd tell him he looked like a man in a pornographic film and he would pose suggestively with the nozzle.

I smoothed butter on my toast. The butter had only been out of the fridge for ten minutes but it was already softening, turning a deeper gold. My knife slid into it, away from the edge where Matt's finger had left its print. Vivaldi was playing quietly on the radio, the sweet tone of violins. I prepared a slice of toast for Nathan, who had hurried Matt to nursery, spreading the marmalade to the edges, the way he liked it. Many mornings ended in a frantic rush; we intended to get up in time but our hands and tongues led us astray. It was an unexpected pleasure to have someone to do this for, this small token of love, readying a breakfast table. I looked at the dark orange jelly, my finger glistening with melted butter, a wedge of sunlight crossing the coffee pot and thought, *at this moment, I'm happy*.

I heard the front door open and Nathan wheeled his bike in to the hallway. There was a flick of the stand as he propped it up. He came through, wearing his Panama hat and a cream linen jacket over a vest. He bent down and kissed me, licking marmalade from my lip, then sat and poured coffee, tapping the spoon twice on the rim of the cup after he'd stirred it.

'What?' he asked, seeing me smiling.

'I didn't even know you this time last year. And now here we are, we have this life, this domesticity.'

'Here we are. And is that OK?'

'It's wonderful, miraculous. But still hard to believe.'

He picked my hand up and sniffed the skin, laid it against his unshaven cheek. 'You smell of us.'

I hadn't yet showered. The print of his body was still on mine. I leaned across the table, cupping his cheek, wiping a soft trace of butter from his bottom lip with my thumb.

'Lucky you,' I said, 'having days off.'

'Hardly, I'm painting the living-room; it'll be like a sauna.'

'Has it ever been like this before, this heat in London?'

'I think, yes. But it's usually a brief spell, not what's forecast as continuing. Little clothing will be necessary.'

He looked at me, ran his fingers swiftly down my arm. 'You'd better go to work or I'll get distracted and then the cows will be in the corn, the mice in the cheese.'

* * *

Cedar End was quiet during the day, except for the hum of Doreen's radio in the kitchen. She was the cook and listened to phone-ins as she was chopping and simmering, muttering at the contributors: 'get real, will you,' she'd say, or 'that bloke needs his mouth washing out.' Sometimes she rang in to join the debate; she was well known to one of the disc jockeys, who introduced her as 'Dalston Doreen'. Her favourite topics were immigration and litter, both of which she perceived as a remorseless tide which threatened to overwhelm 'your actual born Londoners.' Her most often used phrase was,

'I mean to say, it's obvious, ain't it?' Holding the phone under her chin, she would wag a lacquered fingernail vigorously in the air. She was keen on prison sentences and parents who allowed children to misbehave being fined. The kitchen was her territory and she monitored it like a frontier guard, demanding to know what you wanted as soon as you stepped over the threshold.

'You don't have to be mad to work here, but it helps,' she greeted me on the day I started, then offered me the strongest brew of tea I'd ever tasted. I later discovered that the strange taste was sterilized milk.

Doreen was a law unto herself in many ways; she paid scant attention to rules governing the storage and cooking of food; she left opened tins in the fridge and reheated meat several times. She believed that a small number of domestic germs were good for you and built up your resistance to the nastier ones lurking in places like hospitals. Whenever Lucy, the head of home, attempted to remonstrate with her, hovering in the kitchen doorway, she'd rest her behind on the sink, examine a cherry red nail and say: 'I'm not dead, am I? I ain't got food poisoning, have I, gel?'

I started off by auditing the book cupboard in the teaching room. It was full of dog-eared and mutilated materials, some of them covered in obscenities. There had been no teacher there for months. I had little work to do at first. Lucy had taken most of the children away for a holiday in Margate. She left a few mutinous teenagers who went to school and a twelve-year-old, Michelle, who was a pleasant enough girl when she wasn't absconding; she sat and yawned through my attempts to engage her in Maths or English. There were two care staff, a deputy and her sidekick, left running the home. I exchanged pleasantries with the cleaners and the gardener. Lucy astonished me, on her way out to the coach, by asking me to keep an eye on Doreen, who she said was light-fingered and lazy. Doreen lost no time in telling me that Beth, the deputy, was in pieces because her husband was having an affair. That explained why Beth spent hours on the office phone and had raw eyes.

Michelle had spent most of her childhood truanting and was barely literate. I suggested that we write her life story as a way of getting her interested in constructing some simple sentences but she said that she'd started that in other homes a couple of times before and it never got finished. I glanced at the teen magazine she'd got and broached the possibility of doing a brief biography of one of her idols. She didn't say no.

* * *

Veronica sent Matt a parcel, a padded bag, every week when he was in London. It arrived on Tuesday mornings and he watched out for it, downcast if it didn't come before he left for nursery. There was always a little toy and a book in French, some crayons, a plaything for the bath and a card with Disney characters on the front. Veronica's handwriting was ornate, with curlicues and flourishes and you could see that she enlarged it for Matt:

> *Hallo my darling Mattie, mon petit. How are you today? Be a very good boy at nursery and don't forget to brush your teeth. Mummy misses you lots. Next time you come we will have a picnic and go on a boat on the river. I am having your room painted yellow and blue, the colours you chose when you were here. Loads of love from Mummy and Michel and a special kiss from Mummy. Xxxxx*

When Nathan was away I read the card to Matt. Sometimes he would run away when I was half way through and start playing noisily. Then I would leave the card next to his bed. Nathan was decorating his room with wallpaper covered in alphabet letters. I wondered if Matt ever woke up and wondered where he was.

CHAPTER 3

I was on duty at Cedar End the night when Elva Forrest arrived. At eleven, I checked that the nightlights were on along the corridor, walking the bumpy carpet in my bare feet, then set my alarm for seven a.m. and lay on the bed. It seemed custom made for discomfort with its plywood base and soft mattress. The pillows were deceptively plump, deflating as soon as I put my head on them. Everything in the place was cheap and bulk bought; army green canteen china, rough cotton towels, plastic moulded chairs, nylon curtains, polyester bedding in sugar pinks and pastel blues. They seemed to say that nobody there mattered much. I had just showered, but already my skin felt slippery.

The staff sleep-in rooms were on the third floor, where it was hottest. I shoved the duvet on to the floor with my foot. The thin, fitted nylon sheet was coarse beneath me. I would have preferred to sleep naked but wore a long cotton T-shirt; if there was an emergency or a fire or one of the children came to the door, I needed to be ready.

The arid air in Cedar End felt as if too many lungs had breathed it. *Home* seemed such an inapposite word for it. Children's warehouse or holding bay might have been more appropriate and honest. I lay and listened to dogs barking, the faint howl of an ambulance. The building hummed quietly. From the second floor, the children's floor, came the distant chorus of a song from the charts. It was reassuring because it meant that Michelle was in tonight instead of pursuing her boy band heroes, hanging around outside the group's flat somewhere in Bayswater. It was Doreen who had filled me in on the children, explaining that if any of them did a runner, I had to phone the police, reading out the description, which was kept ready by the phone in the office.

I thought about Nathan, the shaded hollows of his neck, the way he kept a spare pen tucked behind his ear when he was measuring wallpaper, how he hummed when the decorating was progressing well; 'Now I'm cooking with gas,' he said. When he was thinking he tapped his fingers on any available surface.

Matt often came and slid into bed with us at dawn. Nathan would groan, 'Oh Mattie, Mattie, early, so early.' Sometimes we made love when he had gone back to sleep, our restricted movements enhancing sensation; the only sound was our breathing, ragged and parched. Then the bed smelled of the seashore, of rock pools and shellfish and brine. When Matt woke again, all elbows and busy feet, Nathan took him for breakfast and I lay on, dozing, hearing Matt's high, clear voice objecting to something, Nathan's patient, low responses, like two instruments answering each other. At times it sounded as if there was a horde of people in the kitchen, rearranging the furniture. I would hear their footsteps moving out into the hall and Matt ringing the bell on Nathan's bike, a warning to the world that he was on his determined way.

When the door banged I'd get up and wander about, sticky from the hot night, eating breakfast on the patio, listening to the sounds of the city. Apricot jam ran from my croissant and I flicked the drips with my tongue. Putting my head back, I allowed the sun to flow through me. I felt dazed with love and heat. Closing my eyes, I would see starbursts of red and green, like the trace of fireworks in the sky. Then I wandered back to the kitchen, picking up a book Nathan was reading or putting my face against one of his jackets hanging on the back of the door. I was still astonished at being there, of having another, unexpected existence; sometimes it seemed as if Nathan and Matt had been waiting for me to arrive, that I had slipped into their lives with ease, destined to fit.

When we slept outside, we lit scented yellow candles to erase the feral smell that sharpened at night. The small, suntrap patio smelled of cat's wee even though we had no cat; Nathan said it must be a visiting Tom. He concocted stories for Matt about a fat ginger puss that came in the dark, played with the toys left in the garden and drank from the paddling pool. Anything in the garden that went missing or got broken, snapped flowers and abandoned biscuits, were blamed on Gingerpuss. Matt listened, entranced, giggling, and jumping up and down when he wanted to make his own claims.

I was dozing and twitching restlessly when the phone rang. I fumbled for it, checking the clock: 1.30. A man who identified himself as Gary, the emergency night worker was asking if there was a bed for an immediate admission. When I confirmed that there was he said that he was bringing a kid in, he'd be with me in half an hour.

I splashed my face, knotted my hair into a plait and pulled on my sleeveless dress. Down in the kitchen I took a jug of water from the fridge and drank a tall glassful. London water had a metallic under-taste. Running a paper towel under the cold tap, I mopped my armpits and the back of my neck. Doreen had left lamb cutlets out to defrost overnight; I thought of the thick, greasy texture of the meat and shuddered. Doreen was of the generation that thought you had to have a hot meal featuring meat every day. Most of the dinners were being thrown away during the sultry weather but she continued to prepare them, perspiring over casseroles and roasts.

As soon as I heard the car pull into the driveway, I unlocked the front door. A small, balding man was escorting a young girl along the path. The girl was holding a duffle bag that bumped against her legs as she walked.

'This is Elva,' the man said, ushering her through the door, the palm of his hand not quite touching the girl's back. 'I think you need the loo, don't you, love? It's just along there, on the left.'

The girl trailed along the corridor. She was wearing denim shorts and a striped T-shirt.

'She's nine,' said the man, speaking quickly and softly, so softly that I strained to hear. 'Mother found dead in their flat: an overdose. Elva called 999. There's just her, no other kids. Don't know where the father is, the neighbours say he's never been around. There don't seem to be any other relatives. I've got to rush, there's a family of five to sort down at the hospital. I'll ring if there's any word of dad. You new here?'

'I started a couple of weeks ago.'

He turned to go. 'Oh, she's asthmatic, there's an inhaler in the duffle bag.'

I locked the door and stood with my back to it. The cotton of my dress was damp. I lifted and dropped my arms, trying to stir the air and the uneven fabric of the curtain on the adjacent window grazed my elbow. I knew nothing about asthma, except that you could die from an attack. My knowledge of suicide was minimal, and what you did with a child who had witnessed it. I picked up the duffle bag that Elva had left by the door and looked in it. It was a jumble of clothes, a couple of books and a few toys. A smell of bergamot oil drifted from it.

The toilet flushed and Elva came out and stood in the hallway, looking at the floor. She was slight and bony with a cap of short black hair and there was a curling plaster on her right shin. I could see that she was shivering and an answering tremor travelled the back of my neck.

'My name is May,' I said. 'Are you hungry? Would you like a drink?'

Elva shook her head and started to cry, folding her arms around her body. Her right leg trembled, the heel knocking the floor. I walked towards her, my bare feet sticking to the pine boards, sweat oiling my thighs and arms and crouched down.

'It will be all right, it will be all right,' I said feebly, feeling Elva's anguish and my own racing panic.

* * *

I got Elva to bed eventually but she was exhausted, so tired that she shook. It took hours to calm her. I gave her aspirin because she felt so hot; I discovered both then and later that grief at first gave off heat. I felt that heat again when Nathan was trembling and crying in Connie's garden. It was only afterwards that a grieving person felt chilly; by August Elva would be shivering, even though the summer was still blazing. She drank some water and I patted her forehead with a damp facecloth. She wouldn't undress but I persuaded her to lie down on her bed where she moaned and turned, 'I want Suzy,' she kept saying over and over in a monotone. I sat on the edge of the bed, watching the hours tick by on my watch. Huge yawns made my eyes water and my skin itched from tiredness. Once a toilet flushed along the corridor and I heard Michelle's dry cough. The dawn chorus started, a tremendous racket of whistles; there was one bird emitting a kind of swooping scream that made me grip my fingers together.

Around 4 a.m. Elva quietened a little and turned her back to me. Exhausted, I lay down beside her and I sang, my voice cracked with fatigue. I sang *Morning Town, You Are My Sunshine, The Whistling Gipsy*, my father's songs that always made the world all right again. Finally, Elva slept and whimpered in her sleep. I slept too, a heavy, leaden slumber.

* * *

I woke late at 8 a.m., cramped on the edge of the bed, covered in sweat, hearing Doreen calling sharply from downstairs, asking was anybody getting any of these kids up for school today? My eyes were tight with fatigue, the skin on my face felt as dry as sandpaper. Elva didn't stir. She smelled stale and there was a crust of mucus by her nostril.

I headed downstairs to the kitchen. I gulped water and told Doreen about Elva as she carried on tumbling potatoes in the automatic peeler, her big speckled glasses slipping down her nose. Doreen brought her fluffy slippers from home to wear at work. The backs were trodden in and they made a hard whack on the lino tiles.

'Poor little waif and stray,' Doreen said, stopping for a moment and shaking her head. 'What mother could do a thing like that? It's a terrible betrayal, for a mother to do that to her child. She'll never get over it, you know. I tell you what, ducks, I'm glad I only have to put the dinner on the table. One of them piccaninnies, is she?'

'I don't know where she's from,' I said. 'Her skin is an olive colour.'

'Oh, a dago then, maybe. I don't suppose you have many of them in Ireland.'

I knew that Doreen wouldn't have dared to speak in front of Lucy in that way. 'Not if you mean immigrants in general. But I might be a bit of a dago myself, you know; my mother's family are from the west coast of Ireland and my kind of colouring was said to come from Spaniards who ended up there.'

Doreen blinked but recovered quickly. 'Get you a pair of castanets, then, shall I and you can do the Fandango. Find out what our little castaway likes special for breakfast and I'll make it for her.'

I left Elva to sleep on while I made sure that the teenagers who refused to go to Margate had left for school or at least gone out of the front door in their uniform. The building felt odd when they'd gone, as if it was waiting for something to happen. Doreen slapped along the corridor from the dining-room with a tray, grumbling that the lazy tykes hadn't brought their dirty plates through.

I escaped to the shower, standing for a long time under cold water to liven myself up. I thought of a mother leaving her child to find her dead and put my forehead against the cold white tiles. I wondered if there was a last note. At school there had been a girl whose uncle had cut his throat. The girl had enjoyed the drama, her moment in the spotlight; she had told others that he had left a note saying only 'it's just all too much for me!' Surely a mother would leave something for her only child.

When I looked in on Elva she was still asleep. I was tempted to lie down beside her again. I opened the window as wide as it would go to try and stir the stale air. Elva's room backed on to the garden and the gardener was there, revving the lawn mower. I was thinking that Nathan would have established Matt in the paddling pool by this time, surrounded by toys, while he sanded and painted window frames. When I turned back Elva was looking at me, her dark eyes puffy.

'Hallo,' I said. 'I'm May, remember?'

She blinked. 'My mum.'

I sat down on the chair by the bed. 'Your mum died, Elva. Do you remember? The man brought you here during the night.'

She turned on her stomach, her face in the pillow. I ran my palms along the plastic curve of the chair seat. Outside, the lawn mower was growling. The smell of cut grass tickled my nostrils. I asked if Elva was hungry, if she'd like some breakfast but there was no answer. I stood and moved to the door but I couldn't leave her. What would she do, abandoned in a strange room, in a strange place?

'I think a wash first,' I said, as if we were having a conversation, 'get rid of all that sticky. Just a cat's lick,' I added.

I touched the girl's bony shoulder and Elva let me manoeuvre her so that she was sitting up. I took her hand and we walked to the bathroom, Elva not resisting, not cooperating, and just moving with me. I washed her face and hands, removing the tear streaks and gunge from her nostrils and eyes.

She let me take her hand and guide her to the kitchen. Doreen was singing along to Radio Two, 'I never promised you a rose garden,' and scraping carrots. She had put on a flowery tabard, big yellow daisies on a black background. There was a heavy, meaty smell in the air.

'Hallo, ducks,' she said to Elva, 'you wanting your breks, then?

I felt Elva shrink in close to me. Her grip on my hand tightened. I saw it all through the girl's eyes; a huge room with acres of stainless steel, an industrial-sized gas hob and an elderly blue-rinsed woman with a gold tooth who behaved as if she'd always lived there, as if this place wasn't strange and alarming.

'This is Elva,' I said. 'It's OK, I'll see to her.'

Doreen shrugged, telling me to please myself, reaching for her chopping board. I asked Elva what she would like; cereal, toast, an egg? Doreen muttered that she could do with something hot inside her, bangers and beans and a slice of her crispy bacon. Elva looked at the carrots and Doreen's quick blade slicing through them. I stooped and tapped her shoulder, saying it was OK, she could have whatever she liked. I asked what she usually had for breakfast. She frowned as if it was a complicated question. Her clear, lightly tanned skin was the kind that betrayed no sign of grief, no blotches or tearstains. Only the heaviness of her eyes bore witness to her dreadful night. Eventually she whispered that she had Matzos and cream cheese.

I glanced at Doreen, who was pulling a face. Sweat broke out on my forehead. I led Elva out into the corridor and sat her down on the broad, low window ledge, perching beside her. I told her that I didn't know what Matzos were and asked her to describe them. Elva said that they were like big biscuits and made a square shape in the air. I asked where we could buy them and Elva shrugged and pressed her cheek into the net curtain. I rubbed my hands on my dress. How on earth was I going to help this girl if I couldn't even resolve the smallish problem of breakfast? I suggested that Elva had a glass of milk and then we'd go to the shop and see if we could buy some.

Elva didn't reply. I fetched a glass of milk and she drank greedily, draining it. I poured another and she drank that too, gulping, her throat in spasm. I thought of how thirsty crying made you, the salt thickly coating your throat, and wondered if Elva would have asked for a drink or just become more parched. I realized that I would have to treat her as if she'd had a major accident, watch her all the time. This must be like being in a crash, I decided, a shock to the system. I felt relieved that I had come up with a strategy for coping.

We walked to the nearest shop on the Broadway, a small supermarket. The brilliant light made me squint; I'd left my sunglasses at home. The woman at the cash register knew about Matzos and produced a tall, cellophane packet. She told me that they were a Jewish food but quite popular with other people too. She described them as being a bit like a giant cream cracker. I bought the Matzos and a tub of cream cheese; the fridge at Cedar End contained only a vast slab of waxy mild cheddar, courtesy of council supplies. Back at the home I put one of the square, beige biscuits on a plate for Elva and opened the cheese. This was what her mother was doing yesterday morning, I was thinking; did she know then that she wouldn't see the next day? Elva ate half of one of the biscuits and drank orange juice. I asked her if she was Jewish, picturing Doreen's supplies of sausages and bacon, her penchant for pork chops. She said she didn't know and rubbed her eyes.

I took her to the sitting-room after breakfast and sat on a beanbag with her. We watched *Sesame Street* on TV. Elva huddled close to me and finally her head lolled against my arm, her eyes closing. I tried to ease her down on to the beanbag and slip from under her but she moaned and clutched my shoulder. I sat on while the girl slept, sprawled across my lap. I watched an old episode of Bonanza and a quiz show. The drone of the vacuum cleaner came nearer but when the cleaner opened the door I whispered to leave it for now. The day seemed to be progressing in slow motion and I was aware of the clock on the wall ticking. It seemed like an eternity until two o'clock, when I could go home, sit in the garden with Nathan and tell him about this lost child. My back began to ache and I propped myself on one elbow as the noon news started.

Doreen had an old school hand bell, which she rang for meal-times. *Dingdadingdading* it called at twelve thirty on the dot. I shook Elva gently on the shoulder and she shuddered, opening her eyes. Neither of us had any appetite. We sat with Doreen at the kitchen table, confronted by plates of lamb chops, roast potatoes, carrots and gravy. The kitchen faced a roundabout so that traffic noise and fumes drifted through. A bee lurched past the window, heavy with heat and pollen. On the radio the Beatles were singing 'Here Comes the Sun.' Doreen ate greedily, sawing the meat quickly off the bone, helping herself to seconds, saying that tonight she'd have just a sandwich. It dawned on me that the meals were made for her. I filled Elva's glass with orange squash. The girl had a potato on her fork and nibbled at it, making no impression.

40

'You won't get hairs on your chest,' Doreen said to her, picking up her bone and sucking the shreds of meat off. 'Do you want that chop, then?'

When Elva shook her head, she reached over and lifted the meat from her plate, placing it on her own. 'Waste not, want not,' she said, adding that she'd have killed for these when there was rationing.

I watched the gravy congeal on my plate, drank water and fetched a bowl of fruit. I peeled an apple, sliced it and offered some to Elva who took it and ate in unison with me. We both shook our heads when Doreen offered rhubarb tart and custard. I told Elva that you could make a face with the apple peel and I arranged it on her plate, putting two pips for eyes and stalks as earrings. Elva watched, wiping her hands on her shorts. Doreen was eating her pudding, leaning against the counter by the cupboard, reading an early edition of the evening paper.

'There might be something in here about you-know-who,' she mouthed at me.

Elva rearranged the apple stalks so that they curved inwards. Then she stood, pushing her chair in neatly. 'Can I go home now, please?' she asked politely, as if she had been a guest at a party.

I looked at her and put my knife and fruit down. Doreen rustled the paper, chinking her spoon as she scooped up the last drifts of custard. Alarmed, I told Elva that I didn't know where she lived. Elva said that she could show me and started for the door. I stood, saying that we couldn't go just now because there'd be no one there.

Suddenly Elva was running to the front door, trying to open it but she couldn't reach the high lock. She threw herself at it, kicking, beating with her hands, screaming for her mother. For a moment I was frozen. Then I went to the girl, taking her arms and Elva kicked and head-butted me, hurting, catching me in the ribs with her elbows. I held on to her, twisting and turning, our feet squeaking on the wood floor. I said Elva's name over and over, trying to keep my voice low. At last she gave in and we slumped down together, wet with sweat. Her tears covered my chest and arms. Doreen stood in the kitchen door, looking on.

'I'll make a cup of tea, good and strong,' she said. 'I've seen them like this before, when their parents have dumped them. It takes a lot of them that way.'

I drank the strong, sugary tea and when it had cooled, persuaded Elva to sip some. I held my hands around Elva's on the mug as it knocked against her teeth. There was a sharp, tangy smell from her. My ribs hurt when I moved and there was a bruise on my shinbone. I was shocked; no one had ever lashed out at me before, another person had never hit me or made any mark on me. I wanted to cry but knew that I couldn't: I was the one in charge.

CHAPTER 4

'Don't you think you'd be better off getting a job in a college, or perhaps a finishing school?' Nathan asked, applying arnica to my shin. The bruise was coming out, a blush of jaundice yellow. 'What's this Elva like, apart from being a black belt in Judo?'

'Small, quiet, lost-looking. Not much like the other kids in the home. They racket around. She reads and draws well. She's articulate, too. I don't think she's mixed with other children much, so Cedar End must be a shock. She fights going to sleep at night.'

'Maybe she thinks she's going to die.'

'Why would she think that?'

'I don't know, it's just an idea. My mother was very ill once when I was small. I worried that she'd die and I stayed awake because I thought it would help keep her alive. You never know what's going on in children's heads. Matt was still a baby when Veronica left but he could sense that she wasn't there anymore. He started throwing things and working himself into tempers. That's what I found hardest, that she could leave him in that way.'

'Could you imagine killing yourself and leaving Matt behind?'

'No, it would be an appalling thing, a betrayal. I never considered suicide as an option when Veronica left. She'd have won then, I'd never give her that satisfaction.'

I looked at him but he wouldn't return my gaze. I'd always thought of suicide as an act of despair, not revenge but then I saw how it could be a terrible weapon for causing guilt.

'She left no explanation, Elva's mother, no note, nothing,' I told Nathan. 'She took a bottle of tablets and slipped away while her child slept. What did she think her daughter would make of that? Even if she'd left one line of love that would have been something.'

'You're making the mistake of thinking she had an explanation. I think that to commit suicide, you must be completely self-obsessed at that moment. You're not thinking of other people. You could see suicide as the ultimate act of selfishness if you're leaving people behind who will always suffer because of it.'

He kissed my bruise, then my knee, his lips travelling up my leg. I forgot my aches and linked my fingers behind his neck.

* * *

I wanted to meet Veronica but I was anxious. There was something about this first wife having staked a claim, marked out the territory before me, even if she had been the one to relinquish it. She was coming to the house after a visit to her mother in Richmond. I found myself cleaning extra carefully and laughed, thinking, *it's not an inspection.* Yet I knew that in some ways, that was exactly what it was going to be, a mutual inspection.

Matt was always highly excitable in the days before her arrival. He threw temper tantrums and sleep-walked at night. One of the first things Nathan had done after we moved in was to put a gate at the top of the stairs; it was clicked securely in place as soon as Matt had gone to sleep. Nathan told me that the tempers and night-walking were usual, and would be repeated on his return from France. I breathed deep as Matt tipped toast on the floor and careered noisily around the house, refusing to clear up his toys or eat at the table. Nathan was tense, too. He threw the windows open and hid his marijuana tin at the back of his sock drawer. When he saw my raised eyebrow he muttered that Veronica wouldn't approve, she was pretty reactionary about recreational drugs. His voice grew brittle and he seemed in a world of his own. His dreams were filled with images of the house sliding on a cliff and falling into the sea below. He twisted and turned in his sleep, muttering; on the night before Veronica was due I woke as he suddenly sat upright, saying 'I don't want to kill you.' When I put my hand on his arm he jumped, staring at me as if he didn't know who I was. There was sweat on his skin. I could feel its stickiness on my hand as he lay back down, muttering an apology. I felt left out, forced into being the one who had to act calm. I drank too much coffee and tried to think of the bright side; once Veronica had taken Matt, Nathan and I would get some time alone together.

Veronica stayed just twenty minutes and refused a cup of tea. 'Nice house, good location,' was all she addressed directly to me in a soft voice but she didn't seem unfriendly, merely keen to be gone. She was elegantly turned out, in suede skirt and jacket with tan shoes and matching handbag, her hair sculpted. Her make-up was discreet and professional. I could visualize her in her flight attendant outfit, smiling diplomatically, that modulated voice calming fears. She didn't look like a woman who could leave her husband and child and I understood that I was feeling some disappointment. I had hoped for someone hard and instantly disagreeable instead of this pretty, contained visitor and reproached myself for ill will. When Matt ran to her and she swept him up, raining kisses on his face, I saw how alike they were and I felt a soreness in my heart that I couldn't name.

Nathan had Matt's bag ready and carried it to her taxi for her, pinching the bridge of his nose with his forefinger and thumb. I watched from the doorway while they stood momentarily as a group on the pavement. Matt was holding both their hands and hopping from foot to foot. Nathan stood waving at Matt until the taxi had turned the corner. I put my arms around him when he came back to the porch and he kissed the top of my head absent-mindedly and started talking about a film we could see in a too-loud voice before he headed to roll a joint.

* * *

I got up early at seven on one of my days off, to dig the garden. I slipped out of bed before Nathan and Matt woke. I wanted to make a start before the heat began to gather. The quiet air still held a soft touch of dew and the sun was mildly climbing the sky. The earth was surprisingly soft, the spade slicing through easily. I heard my father's voice, 'The first dig of the year is the richest, you can smell the stored goodness.' I pressed down, lifting and turning, lifting and turning, stepping along. The loose, dark chocolate soil yielded up, releasing intense, loamy scents. I loved the roughly warm wood of the handle between my hands and settled into the rhythm, exposing worms, weeds, tiny stones and shards of pottery.

Someone here had once owned pale green china. The sun was balmy on my neck and shoulders, massaging muscles that were waking with surprise to this unusual exercise. 'Ah, there's nothing to beat turning the first sods of the spring, all the riches of the Orient couldn't match it,' my father would always say. After his first morning's work he would stand, resting one hand on his fork, drinking cold creamy buttermilk from a cup. He always wore a beret in the garden, saying that his thinning hair meant his head felt the cold. My mother joked that he looked like a resistance fighter lost among the cabbages. When he was weeding and raking he would sing in his flat, gruff voice:

I long for the day I can get underway
And look for those castles in Spain,
Those faraway places with strange-sounding names
Are calling, calling me.

I never dreamed that he might mean it, that one day he would take it into his head to follow one of his brothers to New Zealand, where he could dig acres instead of his suburban Dublin garden. I missed him. I picked up a handful of soil to sniff, lost in thought.

'May, May, what you doing?' Matt came racing down the garden in his underpants.

'I'm digging, so that we can plant vegetables to eat.'

'Can I help?'

'You can help plant once I've dug it over. Would you like your own patch to grow things?'

He frowned thoughtfully. 'What would I grow?'

'Radishes, you could grow radishes and nasturtiums.' Those were good starters for children, with guaranteed results, I remembered. My father had advised me to try them when I was Matt's age. They grew quickly and were fool proof. 'Radishes are crunchy and spicy and nasturtiums come in lovely hot, bright colours,' I added.

'How can a colour be hot?' Matt asked, squinting up at me.

'Because it looks bright, as if it could burn you if you touched it.'

'Like a fire engine?'

'Yes, like a fire engine.'

Matt nodded seriously, picking up a worm and cradling it in his palm. His biscuit coloured skin was sprinkled with freckles on his arms. Then he fetched his yellow spade from the paddling pool and crouched, digging the ready turned soil, throwing it vigorously into the air. I watched as crumbs of earth landed in his hair, admiring his absorption.

47

* * *

Connie and her husband James lived a few streets away with their daughter, Jess. We walked there one Sunday for lunch with Matt riding on Nathan's shoulders and catching at the branches of plane trees. Nathan said that Connie was the genuine article, generous to a fault, with the one flaw of being a bit of a smother-mother. I was a little in awe of her; she was capable and organized, a woman who worked part-time as a researcher for a press agency and managed to make raspberry jam for the home-baked breakfast muffins before I had rubbed the sleep from my eyes.

Connie and James were in the garden, sitting with their guests at a slatted wooden table. Connie was just serving the starter. She wore a loosely arranged orange sarong with a matching vest. Her hair was a shade darker than Nathan's and she was a different build entirely: small and compact and inclined to plumpness. She moved like a dancer, on light feet, turning neatly between her guests. James was an architect and played the piano; sometimes he and Nathan duetted. James was playing Scrabble with Jess, who was naked. Several people who worked in design or journalism were drinking wine and reaching for crusty bread to go with the garlicky smelling salad. Connie took my hands and kissed my cheek, handing me a plate and napkin. She treated me as if I was some rare gem that Nathan had stumbled over. 'I never thought he'd find a woman who'd take him on, what with the absences from home and Matt, not to mention the late night saxophone playing,' she'd confided in me at our wedding party.

There was deep-fried Camembert to go with the salad. James was despatched to make Matt cinnamon toast, his main diet. The Camembert was rich and ripe. I felt addled because Nathan had smoked a joint while we had morning coffee and the drifting marijuana haze easily intoxicated me. There was talk of plays seen, shares bought, school catchment areas and a documentary about Nigeria that someone was making for the BBC. It was all a far cry from nocturnal alarms and abandoned children. Connie told the table that I worked with children with special educational needs, making me sound saintly.

Jess ate gustily, lifting her plate to her lips to get the last trickles of salad dressing, then sat on the edge of the table, drawing on her mother's and Matt's faces with face paints, telling them to keep bloody still or she'd mess up. She had a deep, gruff voice and her fringe fell over her eyes. Matt had taken his clothes off too by then. I was unused to seeing children naked at the lunch table. I imagined what Doreen would say if she could see the tableau of genitalia.

There was pasta with basil for the main course, followed by lemon meringue pie. The food was served on heavy white china. Wine flowed, glasses were replenished. Nathan was talking to a man about the resurgence of TB in parts of London. I looked at his skin, which was slowly turning a light honey from his hours in the garden. It had a sheen from the citrus scented sun-cream he used. That was how I would always remember Nathan's smell: citrus fruits and cinnamon and sometimes the pungent oil he used to clean his saxophone.

Connie asked me about the woman who committed suicide and left her daughter behind.

'What's suicide?' Jess asked, sucking vigorously on her thumb.

'When someone takes his or her own life,' I told her.

She looked at me sideways, dubiously, as if I was telling her a tall story.

'Why would anyone do that?'

'Because they're sad or angry or worn out.'

Jess traced pink cosmetic on her grubby hand, looping it around the base of her fingers. 'Dad says he's worn out sometimes. You're not going to kill yourself, are you, Dad?'

'I've no plans in that direction. I'm going to stay around a long time and annoy you.' James tousled her hair and she ducked away.

'I killed ants at nursery,' Matt said, stuffing basil leaves in his mouth.

'Their relatives will come for you, Mattie boy,' Jess said, sticking her face close to his, 'they'll crawl in your pants and eat your bum for revenge.'

Matt's lip trembled and he looked at Nathan.

'Who's the men's favourite for Wimbledon this year?' James asked the table, collecting dishes.

I couldn't keep my eyes open after lunch. I fell asleep on the grass in the sun, a wine-dazed, dream-filled daytime slumber. I dreamed that I was singing Elva to sleep and that her mother came back for the child, lonely without her. 'You mustn't take her,' I told the mother but the woman, who looked like my own mother waving goodbye at Dublin airport, whispered, 'but how will she manage without me?' I woke with Connie bending over me, stroking my hair back. She steered me under the shade of a sycamore, warning me against getting burned.

She said, 'I've never known a summer like this, it feels as if the world could end. What's that poem, I bet you know it.'

'Some say the world will end in fire, some say in ice.'

We sat together under the tree, drinking the apple juice Connie had brought. Her face was patterned with Jess's efforts, streaks of green and orange. She had a circlet of flowers in her fine hair, which hung almost down to her waist. Jess had made it for her, intertwining daisies and buttercups. I thought she looked like a metropolitan pagan goddess, with her back to the tree trunk.

'How's life?' Connie asked, 'shaking down OK?'

'It's fine. We're settling in the new house.'

'Good. Old Nathan's a bit of a dark horse, he doesn't tell me much. But I can tell how fond he is of you because I have to drag information from him. He's always been the same, keeps the important stuff to himself, gives it out bit by bit, like a miser with his money.'

'I suppose you do get cautious if a marriage has failed.'

'Yes, I'm sure. Veronica certainly pulled a blinder. I know it's easy to be wise in retrospect but I always thought there was something about her — she seemed to lack a solid centre. But still, that's all in the past now and you and Nathan are so good together. You've put a spring in his step, you know. Do you think you'll have children?'

'We haven't discussed it yet. I think I need to get to know Matt properly first.'

Connie touched the bruise on my leg. 'That poor girl, what's her name — Elva? She must be distraught.'

'She's such a sweet girl, so vulnerable. How can I even start to help her after what's happened, what can I offer her? She's surrounded by strangers and she wants her mother.'

'Just be yourself, be there for her, take each day as it comes,' Connie advised, making it sound easy because she would find it so.

Matt came staggering up with a dripping stem of fern from the pond, his face hot and determined. Connie told him not to reach for the fish because they were James's carp, his pride and joy and James would be very sad if anything happened to them. Matt nodded solemnly, trying to pretend that he hadn't had his busy fingers in the water. He had a slight lisp, which Jess sometimes copied, and he asked Connie to make him a head-dress like hers with the fern. She sat him on her lap and obliged. I watched her nimble fingers weaving a tiny crown. She had wide, capable hands, sprinkled with freckles.

'This is lovely,' I said, touching the hem of Connie's sarong.

'Would you like one? I'll make one for you. You can look through my box of materials. I bet a dark cream looks good on you.'

Connie made all her own clothes, and Jess's. She sewed in the summer, knitted in the winter. She said that she hadn't bought a dress or jumper for years.

'Now, Master Matt,' she declared, 'you are the pond prince of Muswell Hill.'

* * *

We stayed out in the garden until late that night, until Matt became over tired and fractious. Connie had made tiny stuffed vine leaves with tomato salad, fruit cups and sticky almond pastries for supper and handed round a fizzy wine. Most of the adults were smoking pot by then, except for Connie, who never smoked anything. James held his joint awkwardly, a man joining in with the crowd, keeping up with the liberal media people. Matt was playing hide-and-seek with Jess. Her loud, rough voice carried in the air. When she brushed past me she had a foxy night scent.

I adjourned with Nathan to the bottom of the garden, by the pond, where we were hidden from the others by its screen of Philadelphus shrubs. The heavy scent of their orange blossoms hung over us. We nibbled at vine leaves, our heads by the splashing fountain. Matt's high shrieks pierced the night and I knew the excitement he was feeling, that loosening of the stomach when you think the seeker is coming close and you squeeze your legs tight.

I lifted my head to take a sip of wine and saw Connie through a gap in the shrubs, a narrow frame in the dimming light. She had changed into a blue and yellow dress and had brought her sewing into the garden. She was sitting upright in a chair on the raised patio, fabric and needle in her hands, smiling down on her guests through the curtain of her hair like a benign, all-seeing potentate. She saw me and raised a cream coloured fabric, a shade of rich buttermilk with dark blue splashes, nodding and pointing; it was a sarong, being custom made.

'This time last year I was in pieces,' Nathan said quietly, his head on one of the flat slabs that ringed the pond. 'I remember lying here by the water and crying. I couldn't fathom why my marriage had failed. I could see nothing but bleakness ahead. It was summer but it felt like a never-ending, chill autumn. Now there's you and I feel as if I'm being sewn together, like one of Connie's seams.' He touched my cheek. 'Sometimes in life, you do find what you need, unlooked for happiness, a little portion of luck or love that someone has been saving for you.'

I was moved, my heart full. The very air, laced with dusk scents of roses, honeysuckle and nicotiana, seemed tender. I trailed my fingers in the pond and dabbed water on my forehead.

'I was thinking, that in some ways, what Veronica has done to Matt isn't so different from Elva's abandonment.'

'Death is the end of hope,' Nathan said, 'that's the difference.' He sat up and took my hand. 'No more talk of grim subjects tonight, I think it's time for a walk home and lullabies.'

Connie gave me the sarong as we left, wrapped in tissue paper. I put it on when we got home. Nathan attached a mute to his saxophone and played *The Girl from Ipanema* while I danced around the bedroom, stroking my arms, touching him lightly as I passed. Nathan had sanded and varnished the floorboards. They were silky beneath my bare feet. The song was as languorous as my limbs. Nathan suddenly threw aside his saxophone and swiftly unwrapped the sarong. He draped it around us. We made love in its cool folds.

* * *

I thought of that night, that visit to Connie's, in October, almost a year to the day when Nathan and I first met. I was far away in Zakynthos, escaping to a place where no one knew me or what had happened. I remembered Nathan's head in the moonlight, the shape of his arm as it curved backwards, his talk of happiness, his touch on my cheek and the warmth of his shoulders under his cotton shirt. I recalled the way he had said, 'Death is the end of hope,' almost as an afterthought, referring to Elva and I wept, thinking that grace came in many guises and also saved us from knowing what awful things might be before us.

CHAPTER 5

Elva was sitting on the window-ledge, inside the net curtain, as I walked up the path. This was the pattern; Elva would always be there, waiting for me to arrive. She had copied my rota down from the staff room and had it pinned to the wall by her bed. She was rocking backwards and forwards, rubbing at the skin in the crook of her arm. She was wearing a faded denim skirt and a T-shirt. When she saw me she gave a little wave. She walked by my side into the kitchen where Doreen was saying goodbye to a friend who had been in for morning coffee and helping her complete the *Daily Express* crossword.

'You could fry eggs out there,' Doreen said, lighting a cigarette. 'Want a milkshake, ducks?' she asked Elva.

'Yes please,' Elva said.

'Rest your bones then. Banana or chocolate?'

'Banana, please.'

'You've got nice manners, girl,' Doreen said, 'pity they had to bring you here, there are some right little animals in this place.'

I poured myself a coffee. Elva stayed by my side, watching me, following me to the cupboard for sugar.

'*Me and my shadow, walking down the avenue,*' Doreen hummed, pouring milk shake syrup into a glass, adding milk and whisking the liquid.

'Are some of the children here yours?' Elva asked me.

'No, I work here.'

'Are you their mum then?' she asked Doreen.

'Goodness me, no! What makes you think that?'

'It's called a children's home and you make their dinners.' She had a little line of white foam across her top lip.

Doreen lit up another cigarette. 'It's a home of sorts all right, but I just work here. My kids are grown-up, ducks, they've got their own families. Only Lucy lives here, nice little set-up she's got for herself, free accommodation and grub on the rates. Fancy a bit of angel cake?'

Elva shook her head. Della, the new agency worker, came in. She was tiny and freckled and vague looking.

'Michelle's done a runner, so there's only Elva here to teach,' she told me.

Doreen was taking a plate of hearts from the fridge. My own heart sank. Doreen had served stuffed hearts the previous week and I could still taste the nausea in my throat.

I pulled a face at Elva and whispered, '*makes me want to puke.*' Elva put her hand over her mouth. I asked Elva if she would like to help put some posters up in the teaching-room. As we left the kitchen Della tugged my sleeve and whispered:

'She won't go to bed at night, she's up till all hours and she'll hardly eat a thing. She keeps asking for you, she watches out of the window all the time.'

I nodded and followed Elva who was standing in the hall tracing patterns on the floor with the tip of her sandal. In the teaching room we unrolled some posters I had acquired from The Science Museum. I was smoothing the corners of a diagram of The Milky Way when Elva moved noiselessly across the room and sat on a table edge.

'I've been there with Suzy,' she said in a small voice.

I turned and nodded at her encouragingly. Her elbows jutted out and she had her eyes screwed up, as if there was a bright light.

'We go to museums a lot,' she added.

'Museums are great places, especially for teachers. They give lots of freebies, posters and such.' I saw the whiteness around her eyes. 'You look tired, can't you sleep?'

She said nothing, but walked to the open window and looked out. I continued with the posters. 'My husband, Nathan, used to worry that his mother might die. He used to make himself stay awake in order to protect her.'

There was a silence, and then I felt Elva glide by my side, her dark head level by my elbow, her breath against my skin. I smelled the sweet almond perfume of the small round tablets of bulk bought soap we used at Cedar End, which produced a scummy lather. Elva's thin fingers appeared on the table by the sellotape, the nails coloured by the crayons she had been using.

'What if I get sleeping sickness like Suzy?' she asked. 'I could die in my sleep, couldn't I?'

I looked down at her. She was even thinner than when she came in; she ate tiny amounts only when cajoled. Doreen gave her doughnuts and cake but she crumbled more than she consumed.

'You can't get sleeping sickness in England,' I told her. 'You'd have to go abroad to get it.'

She looked wary. When she was thinking, she wrinkled her nose.

'How did Suzy get it, then?'

'Your mum didn't die of sleeping sickness. She took too many tablets by mistake. It's quite safe for you to go to sleep, you know.'

'What if I have bad dreams?'

I cut pieces of sticky tape. 'When I have bad dreams, I picture myself locking the dream in a big trunk weighted with rocks and secured with tough padlocks, taking it out to sea and dropping it to the bottom of the ocean. I pretend that I'm standing on the deck of a liner and the trunk is falling, falling through the waves and disappearing to the ocean floor, never to come back.' I looked down at the solemn, sweet face with its delicate nose and long lashed eyes and thought that this was a sensitive girl who had been jettisoned into a harsh world. I stroked her hair, wondering again that anyone could abandon her.

'Will the fish eat the dreams?'

'Eventually, I suppose. Tell me, which school do you usually go to?'

'I don't go to school. Suzy teaches me at home. Schools don't teach you anything except bad manners and how to pass exams.'

'You've never been to school?'

'No. I find out about life with Suzy.'

And death now, I thought. 'So how have you done that? Did you have lessons?'

'Some lessons and then experiences, too. We go to museums and historical sites. You learn things by living them, not by going to an education factory. Did you go to school?'

'Yes, I liked school. Haven't you missed being with other children?'

'I don't think so. Suzy's my friend, you see. We find all kinds of things out.' Her voice was clear, matter of fact, the voice of an adult speaking through a child.

'Would you like me to give you some lessons, then?' I asked.

'I suppose. We're doing Roman Britain. Have all the children here lost their mums too?'

'Well, they're all children whose parents can't look after them for some reason.'

'Could you live here, like that Lucy?'

'I don't know. I don't want to, though, I live with my husband and his son, that's my home.'

Elva was careful with the posters and had a good eye for getting them level. She held them straight while I pressed them to the wall.

'We're a good team,' I said.

'Why would people want to eat hearts?' Elva asked. It's disgusting.'

'Well, people eat all kinds of things. Some people eat ants, or cats and dogs. There have been times when people ate rats if they were really hungry.'

'That's what a giant would do to his foes,' she said, 'rip their hearts out and eat them.'

I heard a gasp and when I looked I saw that Elva was crying, the tears dripping down her cheeks.

* * *

In the afternoon we went into the garden and sat in the shade on the metal steps of the fire escape. Elva liked fruit so I carried out a bowl of dark red cherries I'd bought from the market and we spat the stones as high as we could, wiping the juice off our chins with the backs of our hands. I had also made bite size cheese and tomato sandwiches, nothing like Doreen's doorsteps and Elva ate a couple.

'I'd like to grow my hair long and have a plait like yours,' Elva said.

'I suppose you could. Long hair can be a bother, though.'

'That's what Suzy says. She cuts her own hair and mine. We pretend we're at the hairdressers, we talk like they do. Suzy says, "Are you going anywhere special for your holidays?" and I say, "just the usual two weeks in Majorca." She looks in the mirror to cut hers and I tell her if she's missed any bits at the back.'

I gathered up the remnants of the food. 'Elva, when someone's died, it's more real to talk about them in the past. You know?'

Elva said nothing, pushing cherry stones through the back of the metal steps. The sun moved slowly across the garden. Doreen came around the corner to put a rubbish bag in the dustbin and remarked that if this carried on, she'd be a hospital case. She threw a cigarette stub on the ground and went back in.

'Filthy habit, smoking,' Elva said.

I detected Suzy's voice. 'Is that what your mum thought?'

'Mmm. Sing me that song again, about the threads.'

So I sang, and she gradually joined in:

Silver threads and golden needles
Cannot mend this heart of mine,
And you cannot drown my sorrows
In the warm glow of your wine.
You can't buy my love with money
For I never was that kind,
Silver threads and golden needles
Cannot mend this heart of mine.

Then we sang on until we grew hoarse; *London's Burning*, *Sloop John B*, and *Waltzing Matilda*. Elva sang true and sweet and it was only then when she was concentrating, listening to our joined voices, that she seemed to forget for a little while the sadness of her life, the awful things that had brought her into the anonymous arms of the state.

'Nathan, my husband, plays the saxophone,' I told her. 'Do you play anything?'

'Just the recorder.' She wrapped her arms around her knees. 'Can I come home with you? Can I come to visit?'

'You'd like that?'

'Yes. I'd like to know where you go.'

'I'll see if it's OK, I might have to get permission,' I said. I couldn't see why not; it would be good for Elva to be in a family environment instead of this institution. It couldn't be doing her much good spending her time observing Michelle's absconding, listening to Doreen grumbling about her husband Frank and his gambling habits, going on about her arguments with her next-door neighbour, overhearing her talk of hysterectomies and waterworks troubles with the friends who dropped in on their way to and from the shops. The more I thought about it, the keener I grew and when I painted the scenario at Cedar End to Nathan, he agreed.

Elva laid her head against my arm and slept for a short while. I counted cherry stones and sang, not moving my arm although it was aching.

In the end, with Lucy still away, I rang Gary to ask if it would be all right for Elva to visit my home. He sounded distracted and said he couldn't see any problem, there was no family to kick up.

'She's a real bit of flotsam and jetsam, that poor kid,' he said before he had to answer another call.

* * *

I brought Elva home on a Saturday morning. She was wearing a cheap, thin cotton skirt and scuffed red leather sandals with straps. I fed her squares of warm Turkish delight from my bag as I negotiated the traffic.

She stood close to me when she was introduced to Nathan, who shook her hand and said she was welcome to the mad house. Matt stood between his father's legs for a moment, one arm around Nathan's thigh, peering at the newcomer, then held out a boat made of Lego for her to look at and gave her one of his biggest smiles. They took an instant shine to each other; within minutes Elva was giving Matt a piggyback and splashing with him in the paddling pool.

Nathan and I sat reading the papers while the sun climbed the sky. Nathan lit a joint, saw my slight frown and said, 'just one.' The bushes and plants looked dusty and worn. Elva helped Matt sing his repertoire of nursery rhymes. I saw her relax as she dive-bombed Matt with plastic toys and I hoped that it might be a case of opposites attracting; voluble, sunny-natured, demanding Matt and the contained, serious older girl.

'Elva's found a friend,' I said to Nathan. 'I think Matt will be good for her, take her out of herself. All the kids at the home are older, so she's bottom of the pecking order.'

He kissed my shoulder. 'And Matt's found a heroine to worship.'

He watched the two children for a moment, running his thumb up and down my neck. They were building an island in the middle of the paddling pool from plastic building blocks and small stones. Elva was telling Matt that it would be a magic island, owned by a wizard and you'd have to know the secret spell to land on its shores. Then she asked him if he knew about *The Walrus and the Carpenter* and when he shook his head, she recited the poem to him and he echoed the last lines of the verse after her, 'would be grand, would be grand.'

'Not your average child in care, surely,' Nathan said.

'No. No one else at Cedar End recites poetry.'

Nathan put his hand on my knee. 'D'you think we could slip inside for ten minutes?'

He had been away for almost a fortnight. While I had pushed Matt to nursery and Connie's, he had flown through several time zones and continents. I'd found him asleep on the sofa that morning, still dressed in his crumpled suit. He smelled foreign, the dust of strange places mixed with the whisky he'd downed at dawn to help him sleep. I'd looked down at my familiar stranger and touched the tired shadows beneath his eyes; he hadn't stirred. I ached for him, for that moment when we would become properly reacquainted.

I told Elva that we had a few chores to do and asked if she could look after Matt for a bit; she nodded, looking pleased with the role offered. Nathan and I went inside and fell into bed. I could feel the sun's heat flowing from his skin, as if he had stored it and brought it indoors. Elva and Matt singing 'Jack and Jill' accompanied our love-making.

'Tell me what you know,' Nathan whispered to me later, lying on his stomach, the pillow bunched beneath his neck.

'I know that I've never been this happy, that our little lives are rounded with a sleep and that you can take a horse to water, but you can't make it drink,' I said, replete, slack limbed, content.

Elva was singing again, '*There was an old lady who swallowed a spider*' and there was the *slosh slosh* of water in the paddling pool.

'Elva and Matt are having a good time, aren't they?'

'Certainly seem to get on well. She watches you a lot, wants to keep you in her sights.'

'I know. She's waiting at the door every time I arrive in the morning. It's good that she knows where I live now, she can put me in context when I'm not there.'

'You don't think she might get too dependent, like one of those chicks that bonds with the first thing they see when they hatch.'

I turned into him. 'She sees plenty of other people too. We all need someone special in our lives. I wanted her to share the love we have here, there's so much, surely we can spare some?'

'I love you,' he said, 'I love you and I love the way you've changed my life.'

We started to kiss again, the fever growing, when Matt came clattering through.

'What're you doing?' he demanded, propelling himself between us, his dampness cool on our arms.

'Just having a rest,' Nathan told him. 'How's your island coming along?'

'We finished that. I want toast.'

I could see a shadow at the door. 'Elva?' I called, tugging the sheet up. Elva stepped in half way, fixing pieces of Lego together, not looking at the bed.

'Come in,' I said. 'It's so hot, we were having a lie down. What's that you're making?'

Elva moved slowly across the room and stood by my side of the bed.

'It's a tower for the island, a watchtower so that the wizard can see if anyone's coming.'

'What would he do if he saw someone?' I asked, pulling again at the sheet, which Matt was dragging down as he fidgeted and twisted.

'He'd look through his magic glass to see if they were friend or foe and if they were foe he'd put a spell on the wind so that it would turn their boat round and never let them sail towards him again.'

'That's a very wizardly move,' I approved.

'They might have a power boat,' Nathan said, tickling Matt.

'Don't be silly,' Elva replied, 'this is an olden days wizard.'

'Toast, toast, toast,' Matt was chanting and clapping his hands.

Nathan grabbed him, pulling him close, an arm around me. I patted the bed so that Elva would sit down and put my free arm around her, rubbing her bony shoulders. Elva smiled then, a slow, tentative smile and touched her forehead to my hand. We sat in the crumpled bed, the four of us surrounded by the salty scent of lovemaking.

* * *

In the early evening we decided to water the parched garden. Nathan uncoiled the hose and showed Elva where to connect it to the outside tap. Matt and Elva held the hose between them, directing it over the borders, arcing the water across the rose heads and shrubs. The orange roses brightened, glowing as they drank. After rain scents were released, the mulchy aroma of drenched earth and foliage. I demonstrated how to water the young vegetables more carefully, explaining that they shouldn't be disturbed, aiming a fine spray over the tender green shoots. Matt showed his patch to Elva, pointing to the pictures on the packets we had secured to mark what was in each row.

'Make sure everything gets a good soaking,' Nathan instructed. He was cooking chicken on the barbecue, brushing a dark red sauce over the meat.

'It sounds like a storm brewing,' Elva said, twisting the nozzle for a slower spray on the vulnerable lettuces.

'I'd love a good downpour to wash all the tired air away.' Nathan poured the rest of the sauce over the chicken and wrapped foil around it.

I picked weeds from between the patio slabs, darting out of the way of the hose. I went to the kitchen for a bottle of wine and heard rising laughter from the garden as I uncorked it. Outside, Matt and Elva were soaking wet and were spraying Nathan, who was turning in front of them, a pair of tongs in his hand.

'He said he wanted a good downpour,' Elva crowed triumphantly.

Nathan pulled me beside him, into the stream of curving drops. I screeched, then bent my head to catch the flow, pulling the comb from my hair.

'This is like a rain dance,' I gasped, flinging my hair out, grabbing the hose and turning it on my tormentors.

They cavorted and screamed, Matt's cries of delight ripping through the still air. Elva's hair was flat against her head, like a pixie's, her wet shirt clinging to her ribs. She shook her arms above her head and made a whooping sound. Next door, a window slammed down sharply. We were silent for a moment, looking at each other, then Nathan seized the hose and turned the spray to maximum, jetting it high in the air so that we were under a streaming waterfall.

* * *

During the ritual of Matt's bath and bedtime, Elva grew silent, her former high spirits completely vanished. She sat as Matt had his stories, picking at her arm. Then she asked if she could plait my hair; she did this sometimes when we sat in the garden at Cedar End, her fingers nimble with the strands. I agreed; it seemed to soothe her when she became melancholy. We sat outside, by the remains of the barbecue. The smell of cooking burgers and chicken was drifting across from other gardens; most of London was living outside on these nights. Elva weaved and tucked in silence while I recited *The Lady of Shallot*, her favourite poem, for her.

When she finished, Elva said, 'your voice sounds like music. I like the way you whistle when you go around the home, I can hear you're near.'

'Do I whistle? It must be unconscious. My dad taught me to whistle when I was little. My mum didn't approve.'

Elva smoothed the top of my hair. 'Suzy has a bracelet with little bells on and they jingle as she walks.'

When I said it was time to think about getting back to Cedar End, Elva stuck her thumb in her mouth and said she wanted to stay the night.

'I don't think you can,' I said, 'I expect I'd need permission.'

'Please,' Elva said. 'It's horrible there, it smells and I get frightened.' She moved away down the garden and sat cross-legged by the shrubs. Her clothes were still damp from her earlier soaking and her shoulder blades angled through her T-shirt.

I went to find Nathan. He was washing up and listening to a Miles Davis tape. I rested my head against his back, moving with him as he rubbed and rinsed.

'Elva wants to stay the night.'

'Yes? Well, she could. There's a spare bed. She's a sweet kid, you could tuck her in.'

'I don't know if I'm supposed to, I probably ought to have asked.'

He ran more hot water. 'From what you've told me, nobody at that place will miss her. Can't you ring and tell them? Poor kid probably fancies a night in a decent bed in a normal home. Who wouldn't? Just phone in.'

His decisiveness decided me. I phoned Della, who said fine and went to tell Elva, who nodded, eyes wide.

I loaned Elva one of my long T-shirts as a nightdress and found a spare toothbrush for her. When she was in bed, Nathan stood in the hall and played Smoke Gets in Your Eyes, his nightly serenade for Matt, which was supposed to encourage sleep. We could hear Matt and Elva calling to each other as we sat outside, relaxing and talking, our conversation punctuated by the sounds of Matt running between the rooms and Elva reading him another story.

We slept outside that night. Nathan identified planes as they passed overhead, guessing their destinations from their headings. I held him close, glad that he was in my arms, earth-centred and not high above.

At dawn, I woke to find that Matt had crawled in beside Nathan and Elva was curled at my side, one of Matt's books in her hand. Birds were waking, calling the start of the day. I lightly touched Nathan's and Matt's heads in turn, then ran my fingers over Elva's head, smoothing her hair down. Then I lay, listening to their breathing and watching the brightening sky over the city.

CHAPTER 6

There were times, when Nathan was away and Matt was in Paris, when I felt too much alone. I knew few people in London and I didn't like to impose on Connie and James. They were such an active, organized couple that I felt slightly stumbling around them, especially Connie. Their tight-knit structure exposed the gaps in my own come-and-go life. So now and again, when my official work hours had ended, I loitered in the kitchen and talked to Doreen. She didn't believe in letting people idle about her, so she would give me small tasks to do; buttering bread for the evening sandwiches, filleting bones from tinned salmon. Doreen seemed to me a natural anarchist and I admired her sheer brass neck. She took a great delight in flouting rules. It was how she had survived poverty and trouble. Her first husband had been a drinker who had terrorized her with his fists. She'd brought up four children on the bread line and informed me that there wasn't a trick in the book she didn't know about the 'social'. When the alcoholic husband died she quickly remarried to Frank, who used to come to the house on his bicycle to sell insurance. She found his cycle clips reassuring. Frank made a regular income and was decent to her; at last she was able to give up work in a school canteen. He developed a serious heart condition a couple of years after they married, which left him too disabled to work, so she had to apply to the council and was taken on at Cedar End. People had their destinies, she reckoned, and hers was always to have to flog her guts out. 'I'm Saturday's child, have to work hard for my living.'

Every morning, on the way to work, she stopped at the cosmetic counter of a large department store and used their testers to apply full make-up, or 'war paint', as she called it. She arrived with a matt complexion, glittery eye shadow and glossy lips; she looked more like a woman who was about to start a cabaret act than one who would shortly be heaving the heavy cast iron frying pan on to the hob and cooking sausage, eggs and bacon. She spent her time off travelling to areas like Chelsea and Hampstead, where the charity shops sold top of the range clothes. She was always well dressed under her apron, in Jaeger two pieces, Hobbs skirts and jumpers. On her shoulder swung a Louis Vuitton handbag that she'd picked up in The Sally Army for a fiver.

'Now, you sure I don't look like mutton?' she'd ask me, showing off a Stella McCartney linen dress or a Ghost shirt. She'd smile cockily when I reassured her; she was only teasing us both, she knew she looked, as she'd have phrased it, 'the cat's pyjamas'.

* * *

Sometimes, in the evenings, Nathan disappeared into the bathroom, put the mute on his saxophone and practiced. He might play whole songs or riffs, passages, snatches of melodies. I would sit in the garden reading, drinking cold wine. The muffled melodies drifted on the night air, mingling with the distant barking of a dog, the jingles from next-door's television, the slam of car doors in the street. He favoured thirties and forties songs; Gershwin, Porter, Kern, Berlin and searched in second-hand music and book shops for old arrangements where the phrasing was as the composer intended; he had discovered first editions in back streets in New York and Montreal. I absorbed the melodies, some of which were unfamiliar to me. They seemed made for the dusk and the hum of the city, essentially urban tunes of romance and regret, of loves found and lost, of flights of fancy. Listening, I felt at one with the night and with my life.

Nathan sometimes played to me when I took a bath. He sat on the toilet seat or stood by the window serenading and instructing me.

'This is a nifty bit of phrasing by Porter, a beat and then looping back to the refrain; Berlin wrote this one in fifteen minutes while he was trapped in a New York lift; Sinatra made this famous in his dance hall days.'

I listened to *Cheek to Cheek*, *The Way You Look Tonight*, *They Can't Take That Away From Me*, *I Get a Kick Out of You*, thinking of men in crisp shirts, evening suits and with groomed hair and watching Nathan in his shorts, bare-chested, flour from making cheese straws with Matt still dusting his fingers. I soaped my skin and reflected on the continuity of music, how it flowed through lives and generations, catching and reflecting emotions, hopes and longings, a universal language. Nathan glided into Taking a Chance on Love and I pictured Suzy opening the bottle of tablets, ending her chances forever, slamming a door on Elva's life.

I lay back in the water. Nathan's eyes were closed, he was lost in the song. Through the music, I heard the darkness of Veronica's departure, his passion for his son and his unexpected discovery of myself. It was all there, like a history recorded, captured in the phrases. Tears pricked my eyes for Elva. I thought; Suzy, you must have lost the feeling that while there's life there's another chance.

'What are you thinking of?' Nathan was putting down his saxophone, wiping the mouthpiece. He unscrewed it and cleaned it with a cotton bud dipped in a special oil.

'The power of poetry set to music, the way a song snakes under your ribs and makes you feel sweetly melancholy. Elva likes to sing with me, it soothes her.'

He nodded, holding the mouthpiece up to the light, looking through it. 'There's a sense of things working together to make a whole: the notes, the breaths and how long they're held, the familiarity of the words and the tune.'

'Do you think,' I asked him, 'that if you've been loved just once in your life, totally loved, that you can survive almost anything?'

'You're thinking of Elva?'

'Yes, partly, because she has known love and been protected by it — even over protected. It's the loss of love that's marring her life, not the lack of ever having known it, which is the problem for some of the kids at Cedar End. But I wasn't just thinking of Elva; I meant any of us.'

'I suppose, maybe. It must help, it might depend on your memory of that love, how it affected you and how you can use it. If I lost you for any reason, I hope the memory of us would help me to go on.' He cradled his saxophone, running his fingers along the keys.

'You won't lose me,' I said reaching my wet hand out, 'I'm going to be here with you for aeons and aeons.' I could think of nothing that would part us, I had faith in us, in what we were building.

* * *

Elva always called her mother Suzy, the name she called her in life. I rarely heard her refer to 'mum'. Gary dropped the key to Suzy's flat into Della, saying that Elva could be taken to collect her stuff and to fetch anything she wanted of her mother's. It was a council flat and the council was pressing for it to be released.

71

'It needs to be cleared pronto. She doesn't seem to have any family,' he said, 'and there is no record of a father and no father named on the birth certificate.'

Della asked me if I would accompany Elva to the flat. 'You get on with her,' she said, 'she hardly talks to me.' I had nothing else to do. Michelle had been sighted around Paddington but there was no sign of her return.

I expected Elva to be interested when I told her I had a key to the flat but she just nodded. She was lying on a cushion, watching television and she kept her gaze on the screen. Doreen had given her a doughnut for her elevenses and she was spinning it around on her finger. I could feel the gritty sugar beneath my bare feet.

The flat was in a high-rise block, the first time I had been in such a place, and on the twelfth floor. We had to take the stairs because both lifts were out of order, holding hands, picking our way through rubbish. The heat rose dizzyingly with us and I was glad that I had bought us ice-lollies; the clean raspberry flavour on my tongue cloaked the odour of drains and decaying food.

'Suzy hates the rubbish,' Elva said. 'She puts up notices about it but nobody cares. She says the people who throw it have garbage minds.'

'Have you always lived here?' I asked.

'I think so. Suzy said we came here when I was a baby.'

The flat was hot and airless even though it was north facing. There was the musty odour of a place that had been standing empty. I opened a window in the living-room, shoving against the metal bar that was crusted with layers of paint. Noise from the street below came hurtling in, car brakes, the groans of lorries and buses, random bangings and a steady grating of metal on metal.

The place had low ceilings and was gloomy but I could see that Suzy had made an effort; it was freshly painted white and there were green plants in abundance, cheese, spider and umbrella plants, ivies, ferns and a long tongued maranta, so many that they gave the living-room a jungle effect. Against the walls were cheap but new cane shelves and striped durries covering worn floor tiles. The furniture was old but draped with clean throws and there were bookcases made with planks propped up on bricks. The books were mainly science fiction: Ursula le Guin, Bradbury and Brian Aldiss. There were also a couple of encyclopaedias and history and science books for children. There was no television but an old-fashioned radiogram with records stacked by the side. I craned my neck and saw Mozart, Bach, Callas, Ferrier, and Paul Robeson. No light entertainment, nothing of Suzy's generation.

'Did Suzy like reading about other worlds?' I asked Elva.

She was sitting on the sofa, rubbing her face on a cushion. She nodded. 'This has got her smell,' she said. She buried her head under the cushion and curled into the sofa, her bottom in the air.

I looked around the rest of the flat, a small kitchen and two bedrooms. Elva's room had inventive and creative things, colouring materials, modelling plastic, jewellery kits and storybooks and a big painted dragon in reds and blues on the wall opposite her bed. Her floorboards had been painted dark blue and her ceiling was covered with stick-on planets and stars that would glow in the dark.

Suzy's room contained a single bed, the old hospital kind with a metal frame, dozens more sci-fi books and another wall painting that resembled a cover of one of her books: mountain peaks and valleys and strange craft flying through the air, executed in pastels. She had trained a dense, dark green ivy along the top of the painting, giving it a natural border. I opened an oak wardrobe and saw a small selection of long cotton skirts and blouses, a couple of beaded waistcoats. Bergamot scent drifted from the skirts as I touched them, running my hand lightly along their hems. On the bedside table was a copy of *Desiderata*, an incense burner with a half burnt cone within and herbal remedies for cystitis, colds and headaches.

The kitchen was spick and span, the worn melamine surfaces shining. A palette of paints stood on the draining board and brushes were soaking in an empty jam jar on the window ledge. There was an unfinished painting on the wall opposite the sink, of a waterfall in silvers and greens and men and women in red cloaks climbing a rocky path, their hands linked. I opened the cupboards. There was very little food, a couple of potatoes, one onion, a bag of flour and half a packet of spaghetti. A small table, just big enough for two, held a copy of *The Wizard of Earthsea* with a bookmark. I opened the book and read the inscription: 'To my darling Elva from Suzy on her seventh birthday.'

Advanced reading for a seven-year-old. The bookmark had a quote from the *Rubaiyat of Omar Khayyam*, the one about being beneath the bough with one's beloved. I put the palm of my hand over the inscription and pictured Suzy and Elva sitting at this table, the child reading her book, Suzy watching her, dressed perhaps in the mustard coloured skirt and a waistcoat from the wardrobe, then getting up to add to her painting, kissing Elva lightly on the head as she passed her. She might ask Elva what she thought of this or that colour, did she think that the rocks were realistic enough, what would she like for supper? She would sing as she painted or switch on the tiny transistor radio by the kettle. Then I thought that very soon a new family would move in here and goggle at the odd pictures before covering them with new paint. 'Here look at these,' I heard the husband say as he got his brushes and turps ready, 'I wonder what kind of weirdo was here before us. That would put you off your fry-up in the morning.' A woman who stocked herbal remedies had killed herself with the sure obliteration of barbiturates and a whole way of living had gone with her. Soon the traces would be swiftly erased, the quiet, contained and imaginative life that had been lived here by this dead woman and her daughter.

This visit to the flat convinced me that introducing Elva in to my own home was the right thing to do; a world of books and music, affection and creativity, not the constrained, regimented environment of Cedar End and the well-meaning but meddlesome Doreen, with her inedible dinners and gossip.

I went back to Elva and sat on the sofa, hugging another cushion. The deep thud of a bass guitar sounded insistently from above the room.

'Did Suzy do those paintings?'

Elva's voice was muffled. 'Yes, I helped sometimes. She painted at night, when she couldn't sleep.'

'They look like illustrations of the books she liked reading.' No answer. 'Why couldn't she sleep, did she say?'

'She used to think about all the troubles of the world and they'd keep her awake. The paintings were all about people who were going to rescue other people.'

'Did she have a job?'

'She said her job was looking after me.' She came out from behind the cushion. 'Are you going to look after me now?'

'Yes.'

'For always?'

'No, not for always. They will find you a family, I expect.'

Elva walked to the kitchen and looked in the fridge, banged the lid of a tin and took a biscuit from it, brought the tin over and offered me one. They were homemade, gingery, Suzy's own, I guessed.

'We can take the biscuits back with other things if you like: your stuff and some of your mum's belongings.'

Elva was standing in front of me, her feet positioned on either side of mine. She wiped her mouth and closed the tin carefully. 'You can look after me here. Then we don't have to move things.'

I swallowed. 'I can't do that, we have to go back to Cedar End.'

'Why?'

'Because I have to look after other children too, it's my job. And I have to go back to Nathan and Matt; what would they do without me?'

Elva looked away and started humming. She brought some beads from her room and began stringing them into a necklace, rocking as she worked. I collected clothes, toys and books and packed them in carrier bags. When I asked what Elva would like from her mum's room she didn't reply. She hummed louder, drowning me out. I selected a scarf and Indian metal bangles and a shoulder bag made of patchwork squares in the kinds of colours featured in the paintings, guessing that it was Suzy's handy work. I looked for but couldn't find any photographs and when I asked Elva where they were kept she said that there weren't any because Suzy said they killed the soul.

She was lying face down on the carpet, humming loudly into it, a tuneless, insistent noise. I worried that she might refuse to leave the flat, might throw the kind of rage she had at Cedar End, but here there was no one to help.

Wiping my forehead, I ran my hands under the kitchen tap, then filled an empty milk bottle with water and gave the plants a drink. They were healthy, but drying out and starting to accumulate dust.

'Look,' I said, 'look how thirsty the plants are, they're ready for a drink. I'm glad we came or they'd have started drooping in this heat.' I knew that this was probably a pointless activity, that the plants were unlikely to survive the inevitable clear-out, but Suzy had cared for them and it felt like a small gesture to her memory.

Elva watched, then came and held the bottom of the milk bottle as I poured. Droplets spattered on the waxy leaves of a cheese plant, glistening and rolling to the edges. I ran my finger on a leaf and lifted a drop to my mouth.

'They help you breathe, plants do,' Elva told me.

'Yes, I'd read that.'

When the bottle was empty, Elva ran to the kitchen to fill it, darting back with it clutched in both hands.

'There,' I said, 'the plants are much happier now. We've done a good job, haven't we?'

The activity seemed to have calmed her. I was relieved, knowing that the change was due to little skill on my part, rather that Elva had been distracted. She nodded and went to one of the cane shelves, returning with a soft cloth.

'This is what you do now,' she told me and wiped each leaf of the cheese plant carefully, holding it underneath with one hand, restoring the shine. 'If you care about plants,' she said, 'you care about life,' and I knew that that was what Suzy had said as she moved around the room, bringing a sheen to the abundant foliage. Again, I tried to imagine what torments could have gone on in Suzy's mind to make her ultimately care so little about life. I put two of the plants into bags, as much as I could carry.

Elva didn't demur when I said it was time to leave, but picked up the biscuit tin, cradling it to her chest. When we got back to Cedar End she ran to her room with the tin. I left her for a while, then knocked on her door. There was no reply so I opened it softly. Elva was lying on her bed, facing the wall, the tin wedged between her knees. Her eyes were open and she was rubbing the inside of her arm. I put the plants I had brought from the flat on the window ledge, spreading out the leaves, and told Elva that I'd be downstairs. When she didn't reply, I slipped away.

I stood for a while at the landing window, staring through the glass. Then, for something to do, I scrubbed the tables in the teaching room under Doreen's watchful eye.

'She'll either sink or swim, ducks, whatever you do,' Doreen said. 'It depends what's inside *her* at the end of the day. I've seen it here before, young girls like you working themselves into the ground for kids who still end up doing time or getting into all kinds of trouble.'

'What's the point of me being here then?' I asked, rubbing hard at stubborn chewing gum residue, the teacher's *bete noire*.

'Search me, I reckon this lot need the United Nations or the Red Cross,' Doreen replied, sticking a thumb in her apron strap and blowing a smoke ring.

* * *

Elva appeared during the afternoon. I was sitting on the dry, prickly lawn, sorting out textbooks into those worth keeping and ones for the bin. The grass was starting to turn yellow at the tips and the air was dusty.

It seemed that the visit to the flat had released something in Elva. She was more talkative. She told me that Suzy wouldn't let her play with some children in their street because they were scruffy and rude. I asked if she thought her dad might come for her and she said no, she knew he wouldn't because Suzy told her that she would never meet her dad in this world. I could think of no reply to that so I continued sifting books.

'Suzy won't be back, then,' Elva said.

'No, she won't be back.'

'She used to pop out sometimes to the shops and leave me in charge. Not for long, though. I wasn't allowed to answer the door when she'd gone out.'

'That was very sensible.'

'One time, she was longer than she'd said and I got one of her dresses and wrapped it round me. I got scared. When she came in she said I was daft, she'd never stay away. I don't like this place. I like you.'

'I like you too.'

'Does Matt like me?'

'Of course, he wants you to visit again soon.'

She fell asleep on the grass, her hair sticking up on the crown, her feet in blue plastic sandals tucked neatly behind each other. I watched her, wondering what on earth was going to happen to her. Finally, when it was time for me to leave, I carried Elva in, panting, and rolled her gently into bed. I liked to see her sleeping because that was the only time her face was completely free of sorrow.

* * *

The garden was progressing. The soil that I had raked to a fine, crumbling bed now held dark green lettuces planted a few weeks apart so that we would have a supply throughout the season. Courgettes and peas were established and the cherry tomatoes were clustered in grow bags in the southwest corner so that they could drink the sun all day.

Every morning, Matt came out with me to check things over. I had to stop him disturbing the soil with his questing fingers. He had stuck a couple of plastic windmills in the ground to scare birds away and he would set them spinning. I looked forward to the evenings, when the scorching air grew kinder and we could weed, monitor our crops and water them. Matt nipped broad, crunchy lettuce leaves and ate them as we worked. He had sewn radishes, nasturtiums and sunflowers in his patch, his face serious with concentration. I had shown him how to make shallow drills with the rounded handle of the trowel. He dropped the seeds in with nimble, competent fingers, bending low over the rows, bottom in the air, and a bare foot on each side. He was one of life's starters, unable to concentrate for long, his attention caught by something new: the need to dash off a crayoned picture, the call of the paddling pool, the thought that Nathan was involved in a more interesting scenario. Elva helped him when she visited, finishing off his abandoned tasks; one of the sunflowers was hers, and she had acquired a couple of courgette plants because she wanted to see if she could cultivate a huge marrow.

Nathan was making wigwam shapes with canes for the runner beans. Matt and Elva were busy measuring the sunflowers, head to head now in competition. Radish leaves were coming through and Matt picked one 'just to see'; it was tiny and when he popped it in his mouth he said it tasted like warm water.

'You're supposed to leave them till they get bigger,' Elva told him.

'I know,' he said, 'but you have to thin them sometimes, don't you, May?'

'That's right. Some are a bit close together.'

'What colours will the nasturtiums be?' Elva asked.

'All kinds: gold and red and deep pink.'

'Hot colours,' Matt added.

'You can eat nasturtium leaves, they're spicy,' Elva said.

'I don't believe you,' Matt told her. He was used to Jess telling him tall stories.

'It's true, I read it.'

Matt looked at Nathan. He nodded, 'That's right, you can. That enough canes, May?'

'I think so.'

'They're like little houses for the plants,' Elva said.

'Des Res for a runner bean,' Nathan informed her, tapping the tops of the canes lightly with the flat side of his trowel.

When the sun had slid down the sky we watered, soaking the ground, making sure the little green bells of tomatoes were brimming. I stood back and looked at our handiwork, the neat rows with their burgeoning green leaves, tender shoots and fruits. Tiny nubs of pale pink radish were beginning to nose higher through the earth. I inhaled lush night scents, the sharp tomato tang, and the close, secretive aroma of the soil as it relinquished the day's heat. My skin breathed. On the way back to the house I grasped at thyme and sage growing in a tall pot and rubbed the palm of my hand against my nose. Matt and Elva copied me, and we were surrounded by a pungent, herby perfume. We picked trailing lavender stems and threw them in the bath to make our very own fragrant beauty therapy.

CHAPTER 7

Connie called in at Cedar End one afternoon with Jess and Matt. I was with Elva in the teaching room, making a cut-out replica of a Roman temple. It had been in the flat and Elva said that Suzy bought it when they went to the British Museum.

'We've been to the dentist,' Connie said, 'and Matt was keen to see where you work.'

'This is the children's home,' Matt said, going and standing by Elva, his fingers reaching for her scissors. He was wearing a cowboy outfit and plastic spurs.

'That's right,' I confirmed, moving the scissors out of his reach.

'Why aren't they in their own homes? Jess asked.

'I told you, darling,' Connie said, 'it's because their mums and dads can't look after them for a while. Hallo, Elva, I'm Nathan's sister and it's very nice to meet you. I hear that you like Turkish delight so I brought you some. May didn't tell me how pretty you are.'

Elva took the hand that Connie offered her, then opened the Turkish delight and shared it round. Matt climbed on to her lap, munching.

'This is what they eat in the desert,' Jess said, making belly dancing movements. She was wearing one of her outfits from the dressing up box, a polka dot peasant blouse and harem trousers. She was grubby, as usual, with grimy fingernails, her long hair unwashed.

'They eat dates in the desert too,' Elva said.

Jess carried on dancing, twirling around the room. Doreen appeared through the door; she could never resist checking out visitors.

'Anyone like tea?' she asked.

I made introductions and saw Doreen sizing up Jess's appearance and Matt's costume.

'Been to a fancy dress party, then?' she asked.

'No, the dentist,' Connie told her. 'Well, Matt and I saw the dentist but Jess wouldn't go in.'

'I'm not letting him look in my bloody mouth,' Jess said, 'he's got bad breath and it goes down my throat.'

'Oh.' Doreen pushed her glasses up. 'What are you going to do when your teeth go rotten?'

'That's my responsibility,' Jess sang, pirouetting.

'Right, well . . .'

'A cold drink would be lovely,' Connie said.

As Doreen's back receded she mouthed at me, 'Bit of a glamour model for this place, isn't she?'

'What are you making?' Matt was looking up at Elva and twisting her lips with his powdery fingers.

'It's a Roman temple to a god called Mithras. Roman soldiers worshipped him. They built temples to him in Britain and they used to offer blood sacrifices to him.'

'What's a blood sacrifice?'

'Killing an animal and offering its blood to a god.'

'Maybe that's what Doreen's doing with the hearts,' I whispered to Elva, who giggled.

'You'd better watch out, Matt, you're a right little animal,' Jess told him and he frowned, putting an arm around Elva's neck.

'Stop, Jess,' Connie said mildly.

'This doesn't look like anyone's home,' Jess commented. 'Looks more like an office or something. I wouldn't like to live here.'

Elva started cutting furiously and humming. I asked Jess if she'd go and help Doreen with the drinks. She sloped away, thumb in mouth.

'Would you like to come and visit us, Elva?' Connie asked. 'We'd love you to.'

Elva looked at me, holding the scissors away from Matt's questing hand.

'If you'd like to, we could visit Connie at the weekend,' I told her.

'What's your favourite colour?' Connie asked.

'Tangerine.'

'We could make a skirt in tangerine, then, or a blouse if you'd like. I can see that it would go with your lovely skin.'

Elva smiled, Connie's magic working. 'OK,' she said.

'You eat tangerines,' Matt observed.

When they left, Doreen flapped along the corridor, trailing cigarette smoke. 'She talks posh, your friend, but are they hard up?' she asked.

'No, the contrary. Why?'

'Looked to me as if they're dressed in hand-me-downs.'

'That's casual London middle class, Doreen.'

Doreen sniffed. 'Well, pardon me if I'm speaking out of turn, but that Jess could do with a good scrub.'

I agreed silently but said nothing; it wouldn't do to give Doreen ammunition. I went back to Elva, who had nearly finished the temple.

'You haven't got any clothes in tangerine at the moment, have you,' I said, wiping Turkish delight from the table.

Elva blushed. 'I just made it up. I haven't got a favourite colour but people always want you to.'

I laughed. 'It's like when people ask you what you want to be when you grow up. I used to get confused because I wanted to be different things at different times. Have you been asked that?'

Elva smoothed an edge of card. 'I don't want to grow up. I want to be with Suzy in our flat.'

There was a silence. Doreen's radio grumbled in the kitchen.

'I know,' I said finally because it seemed the only thing to say. 'I put some of the plants in your room, have you watered them?'

'They're not the same there, I don't want them there. I want you to take them away.'

She got up and walked out, shoulders hunched. I picked up scattered pieces of card and made them into a small heap for the waste bin.

* * *

Elva told me that she thought Jess was like an outlaw, roaming the house and garden, free to do as she pleased. I watched as Elva trailed around after her, fascinated, her eyes widening. She saw Jess somersaulting over the chairs, arranging obstacle courses in the living-room, helping herself to food whenever she felt like it, leaving the tops off jars and strewing crumbs around. Sometimes I found Jess a pain, she lacked sensitivity and awareness of others, but I thought that it would do no harm if some of her boisterousness, her brio, rubbed off on Elva. Jess was a tent builder, she was always making hidey-holes out of sleeping bags and sheets, pulling chairs together in the living room to make a secret camp, shoving drawing pins into the furniture. Once Elva realized that this wasn't an activity she'd get told off for, she joined in. I had no doubt, from what Elva had mentioned, that Suzy would say that Jess lacked structure and had a lazy mind. I had formed a picture of life in the flat, a quiet, claustrophobic, regimented existence. There was a timetable for each day; lessons, trips out, swimming, reading. Hardly any of these activities involved mixing with other children. Elva reminded me of one or two girls I'd known at school, the children of older parents. They had quaint mannerisms and ways of talking; they seemed older than their years, as if they'd been born middle-aged and sensible.

It was a Saturday evening at Connie's, the end of another intense day. Connie had made us a high tea of scrambled eggs, muffins and chocolate eclairs. Elva looked at Jess, cramming her mouth with food and ate more than I had seen her manage at one sitting before. Matt was in the garden with Nathan, swinging from an apple tree. Connie and I were upstairs, looking through her trunk of materials and scraps; bits of silk and lace she had bought at antique fairs. Downstairs, Jess and Elva were in a tent made from a white sheet with a table lamp casting an orange glow on the sides. They had donned outfits from the dressing-up box and were castaways on a desert island. Elva had a blush of colour in her cheeks.

Connie was holding up a square of pink sateen when there was a commotion downstairs, the sound of cries and running, a door slamming. I hurried down, Connie at my heels, to see what was happening. Jess was in the hallway, a tattered gentleman's waistcoat around her shoulders, kicking the door of the under-stairs cupboard.

'What's up, Jess? Where's Elva?'

'In there, she's gone in there and she won't come out.'

'What happened?'

Jess shrugged and stuck her thumb in her mouth, speaking indistinctly around it.

'I dunno, I was telling her a story and she went mental and ran off.'

I could feel Connie's breath on my neck.

'What story were you telling, Jess?' Connie asked patiently, in that adult-to-adult voice she used with her daughter. 'Tell us exactly what you said.'

Jess milked her thumb harder. She smelled gamey, of grass and sweat. She put on a low, sepulchral voice: 'The banshee will come for you when it's your time to depart. It will come in the gloaming, a shrouded figure like a ghost. It will give a terrible, piercing cry, enough to chill your blood. If you hear the cry, it is for you and then you will breathe your last breath on this earth.'

'Where did you hear that?' Connie asked.

'It's in a book at school. I didn't know she was going to go mental, did I?'

I knelt down and listened. There was no sound from inside the cupboard. I tapped on the door.

'Elva, Elva, it's me. Come out, please. It's OK, there's nothing to be frightened of. Come on, it must be horrible in there.'

'You mustn't mind Jess's stories,' Connie called, 'she has a vivid imagination.'

There was no sound. 'Please,' I said, 'do come out, it was just a silly story, just make-believe.'

The latch clicked and Elva opened the door, rubbing her eyes. The front of her dress, the deep orange dress with pockets that Connie had run up for her earlier, was wet with tears. Connie cracked her fingers together and sighed. I bent and put my arms around Elva, patting her back. She was shuddering with distress. We sat in the kitchen, Elva on my lap. Connie made a jug of cocoa, a chunky white jug with blue stripes. It steamed reassuringly on the table as Nathan brought Matt in. Jess was scowling and twisting on her chair. Connie murmured in Nathan's ear, explaining what had happened and Jess blew on her cocoa, saying:

'I didn't know she was going to make such a bloody fuss, it's just a silly old story.'

Elva drew in a ragged breath and leaned against me. Nathan dunked biscuits in his cocoa and said that tall tales were well and good, but you had to choose who to tell them to.

On the way home Elva asked what *in the gloaming* meant. Dusk, I said, late evening, when shadows are falling. Nathan was walking ahead with Matt nodding sleepily against his chest. I sang *Roaming in the Gloaming*, taking Elva's hand and swinging it along in time with the song;

> *When the sun goes down to rest*
> *That's the time that I love best,*
> *Roaming in the gloaming, in the gloaming.*

After she'd had a bath, Elva wandered around the bathroom, examining Nathan's razor and shaving soap, his bottles of aftershave and tubes of skin balm. She opened tops and sniffed at scents, reading the labels carefully.

'Nathan's got loads of smellies,' she observed.

I was folding towels. 'He picks them up on his travels, mainly, some of them are free samples. He's got more creams and potions than I have, that's for certain.'

'This does smell like wood spice,' she said of one, 'like the pine tables at the home when Doreen's been washing them. Is aftershave just like women's perfume, then?'

'Mmm, I think it's supposed to tighten the skin up as well after using a razor. You know, I'm not actually quite sure about that, you'd better check with Nathan.'

She went off to ask him and I could hear him explaining about razor burn and nicking your skin; how aftershave would sting at first but then cool your face. She found everything about Nathan mysterious and interesting, a sign of the exclusively female world she had been raised in.

She lay on Matt's bed for the tape of *Sleeping Beauty*. I had bought her a nightdress for when she stayed, a cotton shift with a strawberry pattern. Matt pretended to pick and eat the fruit, rubbing his stomach. Later, when I looked in on them, Matt was asleep and Elva was listening to the tape again, staring at the ceiling. When I said she should move to her own bed now she did so wordlessly, gliding silently.

CHAPTER 8

I always knew when Veronica was on the phone. Nathan would stand, shifting from foot to foot and twisting the cord around his fingers. A little noise came from the back of his throat, something between a sigh and a groan. She rang on a Friday evening as we were preparing for a weekend away together; Matt had flown to Paris the previous night and we were borrowing a cottage owned by Connie and James in Norfolk. I could hear some of the conversation as I moved between our bedroom and the bathroom, filling my wash bag. Nathan sounded agitated.

'That's a pretty prejudiced thing to say . . . no, I don't agree, Matt gets on well with her . . . what bad example? . . . She's a lovely kid . . .'

When he put the phone down he went into the garden. I looked out at him from the bedroom window. He was collecting up Matt's toys and folding the paddling pool, moving slowly. I waited for him to come back in and busied myself with a bag when I heard him on the stairs.

'Problem?' I asked.

He shrugged. 'Matt's mentioned Elva, told Veronica she lives in the children's home. Veronica said, and I quote, "that she doesn't think it's appropriate for our son to be mixing with that kind of child." She'll be a bad influence, you see.'

I smoothed a dress, pulling the zip up. 'What kind of child?'

'From a troubled background.'

'Did you tell her what Elva's actually like, rather than the demon she's invented?'

'I tried. It didn't do much good. She said that we didn't know what kind of manners and words Matt might pick up.'

'I'd have thought he's more likely to learn uncouth ways from Jess than Elva.'

He held his hands up defensively, palms forward. 'I know, I know. I'm just the messenger here, May. Veronica's got a real bee in her bonnet. She doesn't want Elva coming here again.'

I sat on the bed. 'You're saying that Veronica is telling us who we can ask into our home?'

'Don't get dramatic about it.'

'I'm not getting dramatic. I'm astounded. Did you agree to this?'

'No, I said that I'd discuss it with you.'

It felt as if the air between us was dancing with sharp edges. Nathan wouldn't look at me.

I took a steady breath. 'I don't see that there's anything to discuss. Matt lives with us and we can invite who we like into our home. Veronica's treating us as if we're not responsible adults.'

'Ok, Ok, I get the message. I'll tell her. Let's head out of here, we don't want to hit the rush hour.'

As we left behind the dust of London, Nathan played a Gershwin tape loudly. After a while I put my hand on his thigh and he covered it with his own. We didn't speak. *Rhapsody in Blue* washed over us. I felt a childish excitement as we neared the coast and I sniffed sea air, leaning my head out of the window. Our preoccupations were clearing like a mist burned off by the sun. Nathan liked being on the move, driving or swaying with his saxophone; activity, having something to do, relaxed him.

The cottage was like a dwelling from a children's storybook, set on a grassy bank overlooking the sea. It was double fronted, with mullioned windows that caught the glint of the sun. A notice in Jess's writing was by the door knocker: *this is SunandSky cottage and it belongs to Connie, James and Jess.* Inside, in the small square hallway, were pegs with swimming costumes, macs, umbrellas and towels. Wellingtons and plastic flip-flops were stacked in a shoe rack. There was a fusty smell, not unpleasant, of stale bread and brackish shingle.

Nathan ran his hand along the hanging garments. 'Everything for the British seaside, all possibilities catered for,' he said.

The furnishings were in dark oak and walnut; the kitchen had a scarred oak table and a range and the living room was cluttered with leather chairs and glass-fronted cupboards.

'They bought the place from an old lady who had to go into a home,' Nathan said, opening windows and the back door. 'All the stuff was hers and they decided to keep it as it was. The double bed upstairs is an ancient dream, the deepest mattress I've ever encountered, and it's like floating on sprung clouds.'

The back garden was a tangle of fruit bushes and apple trees. I examined the hard, deep green gooseberries and decided not to risk one.

'This is lovely, peaceful,' I said, laying my head against Nathan's back as he reached for ripening raspberries. There was no sound except the distant wash of the sea and birdsong.

He passed small ripe berries back to me and I slipped them in my mouth, closing my eyes. He turned, encircling me with his arms and we stood as the sun sank below the horizon, leaving a promise of pink in the sky.

'I'm glad you've come back to me,' I told him.

'I wasn't that far away. I find Veronica's prickliness difficult. Negotiating constantly is tiring, that's all. You're right about what she said. I should have nipped it in the bud there and then.'

I stroked his arm, running my fingers along the deep curve of muscle.

'Let's make the most of our time off, it's precious.'

'Hmm, no busy Matt, no early morning wakening, no deadlines.'

'No Doreen,' I said, imitating the cook's voice, 'I'm sure I don't know where that delivery's got to, we're nearly out of liver and sliced bread and did you know there's vomit in one of the upstairs lavs?'

I deliberately didn't mention Elva, who had clung to me as I left the home the previous afternoon, gripping my legs, refusing to let go. I had explained to her about Matt's visit to his mother and that I was going to be away for a few days. I was preoccupied with all the things that needed to be done at home and therefore taken by surprise at her reaction. She had burst into tears and pulled at the skin on her arm, reopening the wound. In her room, she had thrown the plants out of the window.

'I want to come too,' she kept saying, 'I've never been to the seaside, why can't I come to Norfolk too?'

Finally, I had calmed her by promising that the four of us could go to Norfolk soon, when Matt was back. She had allowed me to put antibiotic cream on her arm.

'And we'll go to the beach and make sand-castles?' she asked.

'Yes,' I replied, 'we could do that, and eat fish and chips and maybe go to a funfair if we could find one.' As I left for home, I saw Elva standing against the window, sucking on the dusty net curtain.

Standing in the garden, I didn't mention Elva because of Veronica's call and because this was Nathan's and my time, childfree, a time for relaxation and the laying down of cares. If I had told him of her distress, would we have talked and grown more cautious, more aware, and more wary? The seeds of the future can be unobtrusively planted, scattering and taking root in a moment while you look the other way. Nathan's lips were on my neck and the heat was building, my thoughts consumed as my fingers undid his buttons. We made love there on the grass by the fruit bushes, the slow fall of evening dew feeding our skin.

* * *

It was too warm for a fire, even by the coast, but we made one in the kitchen range later with greenish wood from the wicker basket that sat in the hearth. We sprawled on the cracked leather sofa by it, eating sandwiches and drinking wine. In the bookcase was a *Boys Own* annual from 1952 and when we had eaten, Nathan lit an oil lamp and read from it to me; a story about a brave hunter facing almost insurmountable odds in the Amazon. I felt the cosy comfort of childhood: the fire in the hearth, a full stomach, the rhythmic washing of the sea below, the sweet disorder of the holiday cottage, with routine laid aside.

'Is this what we'll do when we're old, read to each other by the fire?' I asked him.

'Of course. We'll have each other in the long evenings.'

'We'll make it, won't we, we're strong enough?'

He put the book down. 'This is a long haul flight you're on, Madam, you should know that.'

'There must have been a time when you thought that with Veronica.'

He nodded and pushed a stick of driftwood into the fire. It crackled and snapped, releasing the scent of the shore-line, a whiff of dangerously wide waters.

'Why do you get so anxious about contact with her? It's not just Matt, is it?'

'I suppose I feel guilty sometimes.'

'Guilty? Why? She left you.'

'I know, but there must have been a lack, mustn't there? She might not have been looking for something, someone else if I'd been there for her. I don't know; I was away even more then. Maybe I left her on her own too much, particularly after Matt was born. She gave up work for a while, wanted to be a full-time mother. She had post-natal depression; I didn't realize how bad it was at first. I came back from somewhere on the other side of the world one afternoon and found her in tears, not washed or dressed, hardly any food in the house and Matt crying the place down in his cot. It's hard to explain but there's a sense of failure. The damage all seemed to stem from around that time.'

Now that I had opened up the subject, I suddenly didn't want to hear any more. I banished a picture of Veronica in a grubby dressing gown with lank hair and dull eyes, exuding a smell of sweat instead of the light scent she wore. A breeze snaked in, making the lamp flare. There were places in Norfolk where the sea was eroding the land, gradually lapping at defences, weakening them. I tucked my hair behind my neck.

'Read me another story; there must be one about a boarding school and chaps who are rotters and the chisel jawed head boy rescuing speech day.'

* * *

On the day I returned to work, Gary phoned to say that Suzy's body would be released for cremation on the following Friday. As there was no family, the council would pay for the service in the crematorium chapel and arrange for the ashes to be interred. I had never heard of such a dismal scenario for a funeral. I was used to a wake and dozens of mourners, family members arriving back from England and America, houses teeming with men in ill-fitting suits, their voices lowered, and flushed women carving roast hams and making stacked plates of egg, corned beef and cheese and tomato sandwiches. There was always shop cake at funerals, iced sponges, Swiss rolls and fruit loaves because the women had no time for baking sweets.

I swapped stories of funerary rituals with Doreen in the kitchen. She was making herself a milky coffee, mixing the granules into a paste first so that it would froth up.

'What a way for poor old Suzy to go.' she said, 'a fry-up on the rates.' She told me that that meant a dirt-cheap coffin and no frills.

I broached the subject of her mother's funeral with Elva while we were on the bus to see the doctor about the broken skin on her arm. I'd been worried about raising it with her but Elva just nodded and pointed to an advert for the Tower of London, saying that Suzy had taken her there and told her the story of Anne Boleyn.

'With her head tucked underneath her arm she walks the bloody tower,' she chanted, adding that Henry VIII was a misogynist.

Once again I wondered about Suzy and what kind of woman she had been. I mentioned Elva's comment about Suzy's opinion of photographs to Doreen, who said:

'Blimey, she comes out with some rare old things; no wonder she seems a bit of an oddball.'

Nathan frowned when I described the funeral scenario, saying that Gary couldn't make it but Doreen was keen to attend. He put down his paint brush and said that he would come, make up the numbers, make it seem more — he searched for the word — *decent*. I held him close, grateful for his offer.

'Elva needs to know her mother had a proper ceremony,' he said.

There were just the four of us at Suzy's funeral. Doreen was wearing a smart black linen suit, a pleated skirt and a jacket with shoulder pads and a broderie anglaise collar.

'Is that what she's wearing to her mother's funeral?' she asked me before we left Cedar End, pointing a thumb at Elva who had on clean shorts and a white T-shirt.

'It's what she chose,' I explained. 'She hasn't got that many clothes at the moment.'

Doreen clicked her tongue. 'What she chose! I don't know what things are coming to. When I was a kid we didn't have choices and you knew you were supposed to show respect for the dead. White's no colour for a funeral.' She looked at me. 'I suppose at least you've got something black on.'

I had bought a black cotton skirt and a navy shirt. Doreen looked elegant in her suit. She had a black straw hat to go with it, black handbag and gloves. She'd toned down her usual make-up: no eye shadow or foundation, just mascara and a touch of lipstick. I felt dowdy beside her. We took a taxi to the crematorium, where Nathan had arranged to meet us. Doreen chatted all the way, telling Elva about her gran's funeral, with the coffin in a carriage drawn by horses wearing black plumes in their collars.

'Men used to stop what they were doing and doff their caps when a funeral went by in them days,' she said. 'There was real respect. Of course, people knew each other, it was all different. Nowadays, the neighbours wouldn't even know you'd pegged it. At least you Romans still know how to do a proper sending off,' she said to me.

'What's a Roman?' Elva asked.

'A Roman Catholic, that's my religion.'

'You got a religion, then?' Doreen asked her.

'I don't know.'

Doreen rolled her eyes, coughed her rumbling cough and adjusted her gloves. She didn't seem to be sweating at all, despite the heat and her outfit. I wondered at Elva's calm exterior. She was treating the journey as if it was a trip to the shops. She took some coloured strips of leather from her pocket and started stringing them together, bending in concentration.

'What's that?' I asked.

'Matt gave me them. I said I'd make him a bracelet for when he gets back from France.'

'Boys wearing bracelets!' Doreen said, 'I don't know what the world's coming to.'

'Nathan wears a bracelet sometimes,' I told her.

'Yes, well, if I found my Frank with one I'd be dead worried, that's all I've got to say. Bracelets are for Nancy boys.'

As we walked up the path to the crematorium, Nathan stepped forward. He was wearing a dark suit and looked formal and reassuring. Doreen became a little flirtatious when he took her hand and I had to look away because smiling would have been out of place. I saw smoke drifting overhead and couldn't help thinking of gas chambers.

The chapel was small and functional with padded benches. The pine clad walls had pictures of grey doves on the wing and orange sunsets. Piped organ music was playing in the background. I thought that it could do with a real organ, some statues, candles and flowers to make it seem more than just an antechamber to the oven. Suzy's coffin stood at the front on a conveyor belt covered in green material. It had a small wreath made of lilies on the lid, the undertaker's gesture. I had asked Elva if her mother had favourite flowers that she'd like to take to the funeral; she liked all flowers, Elva said, but not cut, Suzy would never buy cut flowers, she always wanted them left growing.

Doreen whispered that we should stand by the coffin first and bow to it so we did, Elva rubbing her sandal on the tile floor so that it squeaked. The label on the wreath said, 'from Elva and everyone at Cedar End.' The lilies filled the air with a moist, sweet scent, a perfume that spoke to me of the living, not the dead. We followed Doreen into the front bench, Nathan and I on either side of Elva, the coffin before us. Doreen took her gloves off and folded them into her bag that she kept hung on the crook of her arm. I was conscious of the echoing space in the chapel and the cheapness of the pine coffin with its metal handles. Back home, the church was always crammed with people standing at the doors and old women in black shawls shuffling their rosary beads through arthritic fingers and lighting candles. *I'm sorry for your loss,* they'd say to the grieving relatives, whether they knew them or not. I wondered how you could live a life that ended with almost no one caring that you'd gone or wanting to say farewell. I longed for the smell of hot wax, the light and shade thrown by candles on vestments, the coughs of a waiting congregation, the benign faces of life-size plaster saints, of St Anthony and St Jude and St Francis, the anticipation of something important and meaningful. This place was terrible in its anonymity. I took Nathan's hand behind Elva's back and held it tight.

The organ music stopped abruptly and a man came out dressed in a charcoal grey lounge suit, nodded to us and went to a lectern at the side of the coffin. I had no idea if he was a vicar or any kind of clergyman; he wasn't wearing a dog collar. The man mumbled that we were there to say farewell to our sister Suzy who'd lived a good life and would now be safe in the embrace of Our Lord. *Sister Suzy* was resting now, he added, and I thought that Sister Suzy sounded like a phrase from a song, one that the Everley brothers might sing. He asked us to join him in the Our Father, which we recited. Elva obviously didn't know it and I remembered the Matzos, wondering if this ceremony was a complete travesty. Perhaps Suzy's body should be resting in a synagogue with a bearded rabbi intoning Kaddish, instead of a man who looked like a bank clerk muttering platitudes and wiping his shining brow with his sleeve cuff.

The organ music started again and the man invited us to sing *Abide with Me*. Doreen sang along gustily with him and Nathan's strong tenor lifted the tune. I didn't know all the words but fitted in where I could. Elva looked up at me blankly and I nodded at her, wishing that it would end.

The music stopped and then the man said something terrible. He looked at Elva and asked if she'd like to kiss mummy goodbye. Elva froze and shoved her head against my arm so hard that I almost lost my balance. I shook my head violently at the man who leaned under the lectern to press a button. The organ music started again, *Amazing Grace*, the burgundy drapes in front of the coffin opened and Suzy's coffin moved slowly through them.

I watched, wanting to pray but unable to. I could hear Elva's voice under the vibrating organ and bent towards her.

'Six twos are twelve, seven twos are fourteen, eight twos are sixteen,' she was intoning, head down.

The coffin vanished, the curtains closed. The man nodded and exited through the door at the side of the lectern. Doreen pulled her gloves on.

'Best to do the other business another time,' she said, jerking her head at me.

I stared at her, uncomprehending and she mouthed *the ashes*. It was such a quick turning to dust, I mused, no gradual bonding with the earth.

'OK?' I asked Elva but she didn't reply, carrying on with her times tables. I looked at Nathan and he squeezed my hand, then touched the top of Elva's head.

CHAPTER 9

Matt had returned from Paris full of excitement. His mother was getting married in September and he was to be a pageboy. He was having a special velvet suit made and he would ride to the church in a limousine with his Papa Michel. Then he and Maman and Papa Michel were going to the Seychelles where they would snorkel and make barbecues on the beach.

'Well,' Nathan remarked over supper, after Matt was in bed, 'that's it then, she's marrying again.'

'Why shouldn't she? You have.'

'Yes, I know.' He fell silent, crumbling bread.

'You must have expected Veronica to remarry some time?'

'I suppose. I just wonder what it will mean, for Matt.'

'It's good for him, surely? Makes Michel a proper step-father.'

'Hmm. She might have said, instead of leaving Matt to tell me. I wonder if they'll have children.'

I turned my salad over. 'Who knows?'

There was another silence. I couldn't read it. He seemed a long way away.

'I have the feeling,' I said slowly, 'that you don't like this news.'

'Oh, take no notice of me. It's just rather sudden. I hope she'll be happy, I certainly couldn't make her happy.'

'Happiness comes from inside, I think. Can you make another person happy, other than transiently?'

He frowned. 'Don't go existential on me, you know what I mean.'

I poured more wine, although I didn't want it. I thought of something else Cormac had said that night we had a farewell drink. Later in the evening, when we were both well away, he'd slurred, 'There's always the smell of faded roses about exhausted marriages.' I changed the subject to our progress with the garden and Nathan gradually brightened as we discussed the vegetable plots and the possibility of a pergola.

* * *

Elva seemed all right in the days after the funeral: quiet but not particularly upset. Then, one evening when I was leaving Cedar End she appeared at the door and slipped out beside me.

'I can't take you tonight, Elva,' I said.

'I want to come. I want to look at my sunflower. I don't like it here.'

I thought of the theatre tickets Nathan had bought. 'I'm going out, it's all arranged, Connie's baby-sitting. Come on, I'll take you back in and read you a story.'

'I could look after Matt.'

'No you couldn't, you're not old enough.'

She took off then, running fleetly into the dusk, her elbows pumping. I ran after her, calling her name, my skirt hampering me. I hitched it up and a man wolf-whistled. I ran all the way up the Broadway and I caught up with Elva as she passed the tube.

'I won sprinting medals at school,' I panted, 'but I'm not in such good shape now. Shall we just run for a bit?'

Elva nodded, not slowing at all. We ran on, side by side, the evening air warm and still thick with rush hour fumes. Elva's sandals clattered and now and again she bumped into me, whether by accident or design I couldn't tell. At last, when I thought my lungs were going to burst, Elva slowed, holding her side, then her chest.

I led her to a low wall fronting a terrace of houses. A dusty privet hedge tickled my neck as we sat down. There were dandelions growing through cracks at the base of the wall and Elva gouged them with her heels, snapping the yellow heads.

'Are you all right, Elva? Is it your asthma?'

'Got a stitch.' She took deep breaths, rubbing her side, then looked up. 'I haven't got asthma.'

'But you brought an inhaler with you. It's in the office.'

'That was Suzy's, not mine. That man put it in my bag.'

It struck me again, how little we really knew about this child. She was like a blank sheet that everyone was drawing on. My hair had worked loose from its clip. I took the clip off and pulled my hair back into a knot, snapping it secure.

'You might have said.'

She shrugged. 'You're a good runner.'

'I was; I'm not as fast as I used to be. I'm out of practice.'

'Did you win gold medals?'

'No, a bronze, once.'

'I liked that run. Could we run another night?'

'OK.' It certainly seemed to have calmed her. 'I need a drink. Let's buy something, then we'll have to get back.'

'Where are you going with Nathan?'

'To see a play and I'm going to be late.'

'Does Nathan like me?'

'Of course, of course he does. What's there not to like?'

'Matt likes me. He said I was his friend.'

'We all like you, Elva. You're a very nice girl.' A very nice, slightly odd, tragic girl, I added silently to myself.

I bought cans of lemonade and we drank them as we walked quickly back. Elva asked when she could stay the night again and I said I'd see if we could make it the next weekend.

'Is your mum dead?' Elva asked.

'No, she's alive. She lives in New Zealand. I miss her, and my dad.'

'What about Nathan?'

'His parents are both dead. They were in their forties when he was born and neither of them had good health.'

Elva shook her can, making it froth. 'Does your mum tell you you're the cream in her coffee and the sugar in her tea?'

'No, but she tells me I'm the buttered side of the loaf and when I was little she'd say I was her doty lamb. My dad used to tell me that he loved every hair on my head. Is that what your mum used to tell you, that you were the cream in her coffee?'

She nodded and gulped the rest of her drink. When she had finished she kicked the can high into the air, looking at me to see my reaction but I said nothing and Elva walked on, her hands stuffed into her pockets.

After that evening, I went running with Elva regularly. It calmed and tired her so that she slept better. I kept shorts and a pair of trainers in her room at Cedar End and bought her some gym shoes to run in as her sandals rubbed her ankle. She sniffed them, saying she liked the new smell, and took them to bed with her that evening. She always did that with new things, she said when I asked her why they were tucked under her sheet. Few of her belongings were brand new; I could tell that her clothes had been worn before from the frayed labels and the roughness of the cloth. One of her vests still had an Oxfam sticker on a seam. Gary had confirmed that Suzy had been living on benefits. He arranged for her household items to be sold and the money, ninety-two pounds, put in a savings account for Elva.

Often, we ran once the sun had dipped below the horizon at Cedar End. I would send Elva out to the top of the fire escape to keep watch at around nine o'clock and wait for her call: 'Sun's down!' We took a varied route around the home, including different sections of the park and sometimes the cemetery where Suzy's ashes had been interred in the garden of rest just inside the wide green gates. Elva would pause and look at the small plaque each time, reading the words to herself: *Suzy Forrest, mother of Elva, R.I.P.* Each time she asked me what R.I.P. meant and nodded when I told her, as if she was checking that the answer remained the same. She took a great interest in the main part of the cemetery with its ornate marble gravestones decorated with engraved lilies, angels and raised lettering. She would ask questions with quiet concentration; 'what does eternal rest mean; why does it say sleeping peacefully; what's a rod and staff; what are golden lads and girls?' Sometimes she ran her fingers over the lettering. Once, she asked if I believed in heaven and I said that I did. Doreen had told her that Suzy was there, she said, because God had needed her and that it was a place where you were happy.

'I think God's mean,' she said, hopping on to the path and running for the gate.

The running continued when Elva stayed with us or at Connie's when she visited there with us. When Jess found out that I took her running at Cedar End, she clamoured to be taken too, so I would lead them out and our little group would pound the streets. Jess insisted on running with bare feet because she hated any kind of footwear. We had a formation we stuck to; I led with Elva just behind, followed by Jess. If I saw someone approaching I would call 'pedestrian!' and Elva and Jess would run on either side of the bemused walker. One of James's brothers was in the navy and had taught Jess ship's terms. She would call out 'savage dog to port' or 'beer bottle to starboard' to warn of impediments and she kept up a stream of panting encouragement: 'Keep on, me hearties, the wind's in our sails and there's grog a-waiting for us!'

Nathan called me the pied piper. 'Where's the rats?' he would ask as we congregated in the hall, or 'when are the next Olympics?' He accompanied us at times because Matt cried to go and wouldn't be pacified until Nathan hoisted him on his shoulders and trotted along, a joint in one hand, his other clasped on Matt's ankle. He was often wound up when he came back from a week away and then he might go into overdrive, cutting into our formation, weaving in and out between us. He would keep up a commentary, making the girls giggle and nudge each other.

'And now they're coming into the home stretch and it's Jess leading, yes Jess is making strides but no, wait a moment, Elva has got her second wind and is coming up on the outside while May keeps a steady pace — but my goodness, what have we here — we have Matt suddenly breaking and putting on a turn of speed and it's Matt at the finishing line, yes, King Matt's the man of the evening!' Then, as Nathan moved in front, a delighted Matt would drum his heels against his father's chest and shout that he was the winner.

Once, when we got back and stood gulping water in the kitchen, Elva whispered in my ear that she didn't see why Matt had to win and anyway, it was a cheat because his dad won really. I drew away and looked at her, seeing that she was upset.

'It's just a silly joke, a bit of fun,' I told her, but she sulked for the rest of the evening, reading on her own at the far end of the garden. Nathan went down to her eventually, with his saxophone, and drew her into learning some notes. She had picked up the tune of Scarborough Fair by bedtime. She mimicked Nathan's stance and movements and was bright eyed with pleasure as he praised her for being a quick learner. Matt and I sang along as she played and he applauded her loudly when she bowed.

* * *

James brought Matt back one evening, around eight. I'd hurried from work to drop Nathan at Heathrow, felt the familiar drag of my stomach as he walked away, carrying his flight bag, his jacket held over his shoulder. He turned once and waved, held up five fingers twice. Back in ten days, he meant.

Matt was eating a huge ice-cream, almost as big as his face. James was known as an indulgent parent; the sweets he bought for Jess were a regular bone of contention between him and Connie.

'It's me tonight, sweetheart,' James said, smiling his wide smile. 'Connie's got a bug of some kind. She's in bed sipping iced drinks. She and Jess are going to watch a video.'

'Aladdin,' Matt confirmed indistinctly, his mouth full, rushing off to his Lego.

James followed me in to the kitchen. 'Nathan just gone off into the blue yonder?' he asked.

I nodded. I was hot and tired and still not quite adjusted to being on my own for a fortnight. James put his head on one side, looking at me thoughtfully.

'I prescribe a large gin and tonic, tall and strong like they make in Italy. You take the weight off your feet and I'll mix the medicine.'

I nodded. 'OK, but I'll just get Matt to bed, otherwise he'll be grumpy in the morning.'

Sated with ice-cream, Matt was surprisingly co-operative, requiring only one story. James was slicing lemon as I got back to the kitchen.

'The ice-cream was a good idea, thanks. He's gone straight to sleep. You do know that it's against the rules, though?'

'Rules?'

'Hmm. His mother's rule: she vetoes sweets for him.'

James nipped the rind from the lemon, smiling. 'What Veronica doesn't know won't bother her.' He handed me my drink. 'Connie said Matt's often upset when Nathan goes away so I thought it might be a good idea. There's nothing wrong with the occasional bribe, financial or emotional. Cheers.'

We clinked glasses and I drank, relishing the hit of the gin on my throat. We went out to the patio and James lay on the striped recliner, balancing his glass on his stomach. He had that gift of making himself at ease anywhere; something in the way he moved effortlessly and his lightness of tone.

'You've done well with this place,' he said, 'it's coming along nicely.'

'I think so. We've been working hard.'

'Still finding it a struggle when Nathan goes away?'

I nodded. 'I'll get used to it. There's been a lot to adjust to.'

'Certainly has. I think you've done marvellously.' He stretched, yawning. 'I hope you don't mind me saying this, but you seemed very young when I first met you at Christmas.'

'Well, I am quite young, younger than Nathan.'

'Oh, I know. I didn't really mean that, I meant, you know, in outlook. I was a bit concerned how you'd manage here. Young Matt can be a handful. But I must say, you've worked wonders.'

'Well, we're happy.'

'And it's good to see. Veronica was a bit of a disaster, you know. What did you think of her?'

The sun was full on his face, so that I saw him through a haze. When he pushed his hair back his hand was a blur.

'I only met her briefly. She seemed OK. She loves Matt. She's getting married again, did you know?'

'Hmm, so Nathan said.' He sat up straighter and sipped his drink, rolling the glass between his hands. 'Look,' he said, knocking his ice cube with a fingertip, 'just a word of advice about Veronica. She looks as if butter wouldn't melt in her mouth but she's rather more complicated than that.'

The next-door neighbours were barbecuing and playing Dean Martin. James had something of his smoothness, that wry grin and lazy voice.

'What do you mean?'

'Nothing, really. Just that she was a bit of a game player, one to watch.'

'Nathan hasn't said anything like that.'

'Well, he has to keep all the balls in the air, wouldn't want to load stuff on you.' He laughed. 'Take no notice of me. I probably just never warmed to her much, not my type: a bit finicky and tight arsed. The kind of woman who'd always give you a coaster for your cup. Oh, I'm just one for the old chit-chat, an empty vessel making noise.'

He talked on about a film he and Connie had been to see, drained his gin and left. I grilled a small steak that I had little appetite for. I ate small pieces, uneasy about what James had said. I felt the way I had as a child, when it seemed that the grown-ups knew things I had no way of finding out. I went to bed early and pulled Nathan's pillow against me. I dreamed again about Elva's mother, only this time she had Veronica's face and she was standing on a tall ladder, painting a mural on the nose of a plane.

CHAPTER 10

It had been agreed that we would we have a fortnight with
Connie, James and Jess in Norfolk during late August. The
children at Cedar End were back from their holiday and
Lucy, looking exhausted, was relieved when I offered to
take Elva with us. I had expected formalities but there
were none, except for one form to sign about her clothes.
Doreen and Lucy had rowed over the food order, with
Doreen threatening to hand in her notice. I understood
there to have been some dispute over pork chops and tins
of luncheon meat that should have been in the larder and
weren't. Doreen muttered in the kitchen as she rolled out
puff pastry.

'She needn't get high and mighty with me, making
insinuations. I could tell the town hall one or two things
that might interest them about our Lucy.'

'What things?' Elva asked, leaning her cheek against the
fire extinguisher.

As usual, she was avoiding the other children, loitering
around the adults. She was a favourite with staff, because
of her orphan status and her polite behaviour and
eagerness to please. Often, she was to be found laying the
tables for a meal, following one of the cleaners around the

building, helping to carry a bucket or vacuum appliance, or sitting on the floor outside the office, monitoring the comings and goings. When a member of staff was making the routine phone call to the police to report Michelle missing, she was there to remind them what the truant was wearing. Della called her 'our junior assistant' and said that we should put her on the pay roll.

'Never you mind, little miss nosy nose,' Doreen answered, smiling at her. 'Like blotting paper, you are, always hanging around, soaking things up. Go and play with the others, why don't you?'

'I don't like them. They haven't got the manners they were born with.'

I laughed with Doreen. Elva looked puzzled. I took her away to work on the puppet theatre we were making under the beech tree in a shady spot in the garden. Some of the other children drifted by to look then took off again. Della had organized rounders and the thwack of the ball and shouts of encouragement and derision sounded from the other side of the building.

'When are we going to Norfolk?' Elva asked for the umpteenth time.

'Next Saturday.'

'How long will it take to get there?'

'A couple of hours. We'll pick you up about 9 a.m.'

'How salty is the sea?'

'As salty as salted peanuts, or chips with loads of salt. When your skin dries after you've been in the sea, you can see the salt on it. You can lick it off.'

She licked her arm, pretending. 'Lovely, lovely salt. I can't wait.'

'Don't forget to pack your new shorts and T-shirts.'

She rested her chin on her hand. 'I'll wear my tangerine dress that Connie made. Can I bring my jigsaw?'

'Of course! That's a good idea, just in case it rains and you're stuck inside.'

Doreen had got her interested in jigsaws. There were several of them in a cupboard, hardly used. They were difficult, designed for adult consumption and demanded a concentration that none of the other children possessed. Elva was particularly keen on one of London Bridge, a vista with boats on the Thames and a detailed skyline. She spent hours lying on her stomach in front of a board we had found, peering at the picture and examining pieces.

'Soothing, jigsaws are,' Doreen had said to me. 'Saved my sanity the time my hubby had his heart attack and it was touch and go. They make you feel in control, like there's something solid in this crazy old life.'

I nodded. I found jigsaws as interesting as watching paint dry but I could see how the absorption and sheer monotony was helping Elva and while she was concentrating she forgot to pick at her skin, which was just starting to heal.

We glued card in silence for a while. Elva cut out a curtain shape carefully, her tongue protruding from the corner of her mouth. It was a companionable stillness. I watched her bent head. You would feel so lucky to have her as a daughter, I thought. If Nathan and I had a daughter, it would be a delight to find that she was a child with Elva's temperament and intelligence. How Suzy must have relished her companionship. Elva flicked her hair out of her eyes. She wanted to grow it long, like mine, and the straight cap shape was beginning to straggle, developing a slight curl.

'Doreen said that once people marry, they should stick together for better or worse,' she remarked.

'Oh yes? Were you talking to her about marriage, then?'

'She was asking me about you and Nathan and Matt. I told her about Matt's mum living in Paris.'

'I see.'

'She said that people don't take marriage seriously any more, that it's no bed of roses but no one ever pretended it was.'

'That probably is true of some people. I don't think you can judge all marriages the same way.'

'Matt said his mum calls you hoity-toity.'

I put the glue down. 'When did he say that to you?'

'I don't know, when we were playing with his train, I think. His mum's told him he must tell her if you ever make him sad.'

I shivered in the heat. This was a strange and unexpected ambush. Elva was finishing her cutting, holding it up to check the edges.

I cleared my throat. 'I'd never make Matt sad, I hope. I don't think it's a very nice thing for his mum to have said. Was he worried?'

Elva shrugged. 'Don't know. Will he bring his tapes to Norfolk, so we can listen in bed?'

'Mmm? Yes, of course. He always takes them with him.' I thought of Veronica, standing in our house, elegant and guarded. Matt was with her until the end of the week, returning on Friday just before our own holiday. I wondered what she was saying to him, what anxieties she was causing. Nathan had spoken to her about her edict on Elva but she hadn't let the matter drop. There had been a letter from her in the last week on personalized notepaper; it was typed, rather official looking. She had deliberately not emailed it, I thought; the dark printed letters ensured distance. I found the tone pompous, although I hadn't voiced this to Nathan.

Dear Nathan,

I am not at all happy about this situation with Elva, the child from the children's home spending time with Matt. I had hoped that you would be reasonable and try to accept my viewpoint but it seems that this is not the case. I am only thinking of my little boy's welfare and I am surprised that you are not doing the same. I cannot accept your statement about Matt mixing with all kinds of children at school: school is not within

111

your jurisdiction, whereas who visits your home is. Matt is at a very impressionable and tender age. I do not think he should be worrying about topics such as death and violence. He mentioned that Elva had spoken of a child whose father had hit her and bruised her arm — presumably one of the other inmates of the establishment where she lives. Do you honestly think that these are suitable things for our son to be hearing? I do hope that you will be able to meet me half way on this matter. We always said that we would try to put Matt first, whatever our differences. I have discussed all of this with Michel and he agrees that it is not good for Matt's welfare to have him mixing with this kind of unfortunate child. I do not want to have to seek any kind of legal redress over your intransigence. I know that deep down, you will know that what I am saying is right, whatever others might be urging you to think.
Best wishes, V.

The first thing that occurred to me when I read it was: *how odd, to send best wishes to someone you have just been threatening.* The second was that I was presumably this 'other' who was allegedly influencing Nathan. I wanted to laugh, a mixture of nerves and anger but Nathan's taut expression stopped me. He swore viciously and poured himself a large whisky. We discussed what Veronica might mean by 'legal redress'. Taking Matt away to Paris to live, Nathan said, that's what she was implying. She'd probably have a good case for all he knew, being the mother. I had agreed to talk to Elva and ask her not to mention anything about what went on in the children's home to Matt. Gloom had settled over us that evening. We were carefully polite with each other, a behaviour that is enervating between two people who are usually intimate. Nathan vanished to the bedroom and played his saxophone while I attempted to read. I gave up after a while and watched a detective series on the television.

* * *

Elva was humming *Here Comes the Sun*. It was being played constantly on the radio, echoing from the kitchen all the way through the building. I was suddenly thirsty. I went to the kitchen for water, my bare feet kicking up powdery dust from the parched grass. Doreen was there, reading her stars in the paper, listening to a chat show. The topic was whether it's better to tell white lies instead of hurting a person's feelings.

'Might as well have stayed in bed this morning,' Doreen said, jabbing a finger at her paper. 'I'm going to have an argument that will cloud things for a few days. Lucy's going to be on the warpath, no doubt. This is *my* kitchen so she'd better watch her mouth when she comes swanning in here. You all right, ducks?' she asked me, 'you look hot, don't stay out there too long.'

I nodded. The water was lukewarm, brackish tasting. I drank deeply but it didn't quench my thirst.

I went back to Elva and sat next to her. 'Can I ask you a big favour?'

She looked up at me with her serious expression. 'Yes.'

'When you're with Matt, can you not tell him too much about the children's home and the things that happen here. Especially some of the difficult things that have happened to other children.'

'Why?'

I hesitated. 'Well, he's very young and he might not understand. His mummy might not understand either.'

Elva shook the glue and spread a line carefully on a clown's hat. She pressed the card seam together dextrously.

'Matt's mum doesn't like you, does she?'

'No, I don't think she does.'

'Why?'

113

'I'm not sure. It doesn't really matter, Elva. Grownups sometimes don't get on. It's not for you to worry about.'

'Suzy says people shouldn't fuss and fight. She says that the smile you give out is the smile that comes back to you.'

'That's a lovely way to look at life. It's a lovely way to remember your mum.'

'When will my hair be as long as yours?'

'I should think it'll take a couple of months.' I was about to say around Christmas but stopped myself. I didn't want to mention Christmas in case Elva asked where she would be spending it. I rubbed the heels of my hands in my eyes. Words suddenly seemed to have become heavily laden with potential trip wires, little detonators that could ambush unexpectedly.

* * *

The hot sun tracked us to Norfolk, burning the tarmac. Matt and Elva sat in the back of our car. Elva had her very own saxophone propped beside her. Nathan had bought it for her, along with a starter book for learning to read music. She had already cleaned the instrument twice before we set out. As we exited from London we sang along to songs on Matt's tapes. We all joined in with his current favourite several times, at his insistence:

> *Whether the weather be cold*
> *Or whether the weather be hot*
> *Whether the weather be fine*
> *Or whether the weather be not*
> *We'll weather the weather*
> *Whatever the weather*
> *Whether we like it or not!*

Matt was on what Nathan called 'fast forward' after his time in Paris: edgy, talking loudly, finding it hard to sit still. He smelled different after he'd been away, of peaches and pears. I think it was the fabric softener that Veronica used on his clothes. Nathan said that she'd always been a great one for plug-in air fresheners, scented candles and the like. Matt had returned with several new outfits, beautiful fabrics, designer labels. He looked a real little French boy with his pleated shorts and tops with side shoulder buttons. When I'd gone to kiss him as he arrived home, he'd ducked under my arm and clattered to the kitchen, asking for brioche. Nathan told him we didn't have brioche and offered him his usual toast. He sat on the floor and crumpled, crying angrily. Nathan sat next to him, stroking his hair. When he calmed down, Nathan took him to the supermarket where they bought several brioche loaves to go with the dark chocolate drink he'd brought back in his case. Veronica had put a label on the side of the tin: *Mattie likes just a teaspoon made with half water & half skimmed-milk. Bon nuit, man petit choufleur!*

'So,' Nathan said, spooning out a careful teaspoon, 'you're a little cauliflower! I think you're more of a turnip, or maybe a radish?'

'If Daddy was a vegetable, I think he'd be a carrot, because of his hair,' I said.

Matt had laughed warily, stabbing a knife into the butter.

We travelled in a convoy, stopping at service stations for bottles of cold water. Connie encouraged the children to eat bananas, saying that they were light on the stomach and nutritious. Matt pretended that his was a gun, standing with his legs apart and taking aim. Elva ate hers daintily, breaking small pieces off and folding the skin afterwards. The skins made good plant compost, she told Connie, Suzy put them around the bottom of the house-plants sometimes to give them a boost. I caught Jess placing her banana skin on the car park path, hoping that someone would slip. She scowled when I remonstrated with her and dug her hands into her pockets. I couldn't help laughing. She reminded me of one of those naughty girls in comic books: Beryl the Peril or Minnie the Minx. Doreen would say, 'She's no better than she ought to be, that one, she needs a good clip round the ear and sent to bed without any supper.'

Back in the car, Elva asked anxiously, 'Oh, what about our garden? The flowers and vegetables will die without water.'

'All taken care of,' Nathan told her. 'The neighbours at sixty-five are going to water so don't worry.'

I hoped we didn't need to. Their idea of watering might not be ours and the plants would need a nightly saturation in this weather. Oh stop it, I told myself, it will be OK, they won't let things die.

As we approached the coast, Elva grew quiet. She leaned forward in her seat and tucked a hot hand under my hair. I could feel the beat of her pulse on my neck, a faint drum beat of expectation. When we turned off the road in to the driveway of the cottage, she whispered into my ear:

'It's like a house from *The Wind in the Willows*.'

I whispered back, 'I know, I think maybe mole sleeps here sometimes.'

Before we could unload the cars, the children clamoured to go down to the sea. The tide was in, running quiet and full. We abandoned the chores and kicked our shoes off. The children streamed ahead of us. Jess held her arms out, making aeroplane noises, wheeling from side to side. Matt copied her, stumbling determinedly in her wake. Elva ran in a straight line, noiselessly, hands at her sides. She looked like a speeding Irish dancer. As I watched she reached the waves and carried on running, straight in, up to her chest. She turned, swaying, an expression of startled delight on her face. Her tangerine dress billowed out around her like a bright sail.

'She can't swim!' I shouted at Nathan.

'It's OK, it shelves very gradually,' he called back, laughing.

Jess threw off her T-shirt. 'You twit, Elva, you're supposed to take your clothes off first!'

'Twit Elva,' Matt echoed.

'I'm a fish! I'm a fish!' Elva yelled, splashing. 'The sea is big and I'm a fish!' She scooped up handfuls of water and licked her arm, a long sweeping lick. 'Oh, it *is* salty!'

* * *

There was the tiniest of breezes during the day. The sea drifted placidly to the shore, a warm milky green. We emerged into the mornings gradually. Tranquillity was all around us: the wide sky, the endless, empty beach, the slow routine of people with nothing to do but enjoy the contented world, yet Nathan was restless during the nights, muttering and scratching in his sleep. Sometimes I woke and saw his silhouette against the window and smelled the pungent smoke from his joint. Then I might slip from bed and go to him, placing a hand on his arm. His skin was dry and smooth, scrubbed by the sea. He would kiss my forehead and tell me to go back to sleep, he was just doing a bit of thinking, nothing to fret over. I stayed where I was, saying nothing, apprehension paralysing me. He slept heavily after dawn, his hand squeezing and bunching the pillow under his chin.

I was waking early. I thought it was the utter silence that roused me. Having been a city dweller all my life, I was used to the lulling hinterland of constant stirrings. I loved wandering in my nightdress into the living-room, pushing back the wooden shutters and sitting on the window seat with my coffee. The sun idled on the fruit bushes, burning off the dew. In the distance, the sea glinted, the tide sucking the shore. The hazelnut steam from my cup scented the air. Soon after I settled, Elva would appear, fetch croissants and jam from the kitchen and lie along my stretched legs. Her head propped on one hand, she munched her way through the croissants, taking sips of my coffee. Her appetite was growing and she craved sweet things: puddings, biscuits, sugary cakes. When she had finished this first breakfast she placed her head on my chest and played with the lace on my sleeve. We sat in silence until Matt erupted. One morning, I heard him calling confusedly for *'Maman!'* and I must have winced.

'You're not *Maman,'* Elva whispered, 'you're my May.'

Once everyone had been roused by Matt's racket, the children played in the back garden while we made scrambled eggs and toasted muffins. Jess had brought a tent and this was made into an outdoor den. Jess and Elva ferried their breakfast out there on a yellow plastic picnic set; a jug of orange juice, plates of eggs and brioche for Matt. He trotted alongside them with cutlery. He had taken to constantly wearing a canvas bag that he'd brought back from Paris, slung bandoleer style across his shoulder. It banged against his hip, rattling with small toys. It looked vaguely military and he said that Papa Michel had used it in the scouts. Veronica had sewn his name on to the front in navy embroidery thread: *Matthew Erskine.*

Towards the end of our first week, the languid flow of hours worked their magic and we settled into the rhythm of slow contentment. I watched Nathan's brow relax and felt the reassurance of the bond between us. Our pores had opened, breathing in the salt. The children glowed, turning that light nut butter shade that you only ever see on youthful skin. When they came close, I could smell warm sand and the briny, mysterious scents of the rock pools where they spent hours trawling with their buckets.

Matt had promised his mother a shell collection and he circled the beach, gathering intently, discarding any broken specimens. He washed and polished those that passed muster and wrapped them in a soft cloth. During his hunting he found an empty shampoo bottle with Cyrillic lettering. Nathan told him that it was Russian and we wondered who might have used it and where. Elva said it must have been a Cossack, riding the wild steppes but James commented that Cossacks were manly men and never washed their hair, but covered it in goose grease against the icy cold.

When the afternoon sun was too high for comfort, we took an hour's siesta, sprawled on sofas and chairs. James played the piano for a while in little fits and starts; snatches of Chopin and Schubert. Sometimes he accompanied Elva as she played *Three Blind Mice* on her saxophone and the adults would all clap. Connie told her that she had a real gift and she beamed, holding the instrument tight to her chest. Then Elva would turn to her jigsaw, which she had set out on a tray. She was working her way around the edges. Jess might help her for a short while but she didn't have the patience for it and would wander away to her den. Matt dozed on Nathan's lap, his bag clutched under his arm while I read and Connie worked on a piece of embroidery for the neck of a dress. I would snooze briefly, listening to James's chords and have vivid semi-wakening dreams, flashes of bright scenes that vanished as soon as I jolted awake.

We ate simply and well; fish, bread and salads. I bought cakes, with Elva in mind; if it was comfort food, as far as I was concerned, she should eat as many as she wanted. There was a tiny fish shop a mile away, just above the sands and Nathan walked there with Matt every morning to get the day's catch. They came back with parcels wrapped in white paper, which they would open and spill on to the kitchen table. The fishmonger threw handfuls of herbs in and the delicate fronds of parsley and dill glistened greenly against the fat cod, pale silky plaice or yellow smoked haddock whose colour reminded me of the nicotine aged ceilings of some Dublin pubs. The four adults would then look at recipes and decide how the fish should be prepared. James liked pastry casings and sauces; Connie and Nathan favoured simply grilled dishes. I preferred fish poached in a little milk, with bay leaves and potatoes, the way it had always been prepared back home. We took turns with the cooking, experimenting and inventing. James said that we should cash in on the vogue for cookery books and write one; we could call it *Sun and Sky Suppers*. Nathan must have talked to Connie about Veronica's letter because she came up to me as I was preparing dinner one evening and told me not to worry. Veronica was full of hot air, she said, probably getting all worked up because of her wedding. Nathan would never give up Matt. We just had to ride the waves and wait for her to calm down.

'You really think so?' I looked at Connie's confident eyes, her sturdy, reassuring shoulders.

'Absolutely,' Connie confirmed. 'This will all pass, given time. Old Veronica can erupt now and again but she has a short attention span, believe me. And of course, you can't discount the fact that she must feel guilty that she abandoned Matt. Guilt can make people angry. Maybe she's trying to justify something to herself. I've told Nathan the same and I've told him that he ought to be concentrating on you, not Veronica's foot stamping.'

I whisked a salad dressing with lighter fingers and heart. It always lifts the spirits to be told what you want to hear. I'd had those thoughts about Veronica's guilt myself. Connie meant well. Because she had a generous, uncomplicated nature, she couldn't read or foresee complexity in others. I couldn't blame Connie in any way afterwards. She was rooting for Nathan and me, an understandable partisanship.

We took the kitchen table outside to a shady spot and ate in the back garden; salmon coated in lemons, with small waxy potatoes smothered in herb butter and the salad of dark leaves with shreds of spicy radish. After a busy day in the sun the children were ravenous and quiet. When their stomachs were full they got a second wind and started hide-and-seek. We lit candles to illuminate the descending dusk, opened another bottle of wine and sank back into our chairs.

'She's a lovely little kid,' James motioned with his glass as Elva's skinny brown legs darted around a corner. 'It's good to see her coming out of herself, eating well. Pity Veronica can't meet her properly, it might put a stop to all this nonsense.'

I glanced at Nathan. 'I'm not convinced that Elva's really the problem,' I said.

'Oh?' James asked. 'Say more.'

I hesitated, took a drink. 'I wondered if maybe Elva's just an excuse that Veronica's using. She may not be keen on the idea of Nathan, myself and Matt as a family unit.'

'Oh, surely not,' Connie said. 'I don't think she's jealous in that way.'

'Nathan, what do you reckon?' James asked.

Yes, Nathan, I thought, what do you reckon, I would like to know. The subject of Veronica was like a somnolent tiger, lying between us, and both of us wary of rousing it.

He poured himself another brimming glass of wine. His eyes were unfocused. 'I think,' he said slowly, 'that I'm the last person to ask. I don't know Veronica now. She's a stranger. I expect May's right: she's studied all that psychology, she knows what makes people tick better than I do.'

For the first time since I had known Nathan, I felt truly angry with him, a flare of emotion, bright and quick like the candle flame. He was passing the buck.

'You have to try and understand someone's motives to deal with them, in a situation like this,' I said tightly.

He looked at me blankly. 'Maybe there isn't anything to understand. You think too much sometimes, make too much of things.'

'Well, thanks for the vote of confidence,' I said.

'That's not fair, Nathan,' Connie reproved him. 'This can't be easy for May.'

'I didn't say it was, but there's no need to make it more complicated than it is. Women always think that talking about things makes them better. Sometimes it bloody well doesn't.'

'Come on, boys and girls, it's too hot to argue,' James said.

'You asked me,' Nathan told him, thumping his glass down. Wine slopped on to the table, forming a shining pond in the candlelight.

Connie lifted a lump of wax on her fingertip and placed it on the candle base. 'If Veronica is trying to cause trouble between you, she's certainly succeeding.'

'Oh, leave it, Con, it's not *your* child who might be taken from you,' Nathan said roughly.

I saw the fear in his eyes then. I took some plates and left the table, carrying them into the welcome dark of the kitchen. I felt as if something was slipping from my grasp. I scraped salmon scales into the bin. The fishy smell was suddenly rank and nauseating.

The curtain moved and I turned, startled. Elva slipped out beside me.

'I haven't had pudding yet,' she said, holding my arm in a tight grip.

'Aren't you supposed to be hiding?' I wondered how much she'd heard.

'I don't want to play that any more. Why is Nathan so cross?'

'He's tired, that's all.'

'Is Matt going to live in France?' She rubbed her face on my arm.

I crouched down. 'No, he isn't. There are just a few problems, Elva. Nothing for you to worry about.'

'I've never been to France.'

'Do you know, neither have I. Maybe we can go there one day. Now, apple cake or a meringue, which is it to be?'

We went back out to the table with the puddings. Elva stayed by me for the rest of the evening. At bedtime, after several stories, she wanted me to stay with her until she fell asleep. I slept too, my head on the edge of her pillow, waking when Nathan shook my shoulder.

'I'm sorry,' he whispered, lifting me up. 'Come and have a night cap, everyone else is in bed.'

The house was still. We sat outside with whisky, contemplating the stars.

'We've got to sort this out,' I said.

'I know, I'll write tomorrow. I've been pretending it will go away. That's not fair on any of us.'

We exchanged smoky whisky kisses and lay on the grass, our arms touching, breathing together, and the faint drone of Matt's story tape the only sound in the sleeping night.

'Tell me what you know,' Nathan whispered, nibbling my ear.

'I know that going out with wet hair means you get a cold, that it's too late to sharpen the sword when the drum beats for battle and that if your palm itches you'll come into money,' I told him.

In a corner of my mind I had a flickering, panicky realization that perhaps what I did know just wasn't enough to help me navigate the terrain we had wandered into.

CHAPTER 11

We were in the garden in the early evening, that in-between, fatigued time of day when children become cranky and adults' thoughts turn to a gin and tonic or glass of wine. I was sipping gin, a slice of lime bobbing at the rim of the glass. Nathan was sitting on the grass with Elva, listening to her practising her daily scales on the saxophone. They were both cross-legged and intent. He occasionally put his hand out and adjusted her fingers on the taps. When his phone rang, he glanced at the screen, frowned, and told her to keep playing, he wouldn't be long.

I watched her focusing on her fingers, her brow furrowed with concentration. She and Jess had taken to braiding the front of their hair so that it stood up at the front, like little antennae. My eyes flickered to Nathan, pacing amongst the rhododendrons at the far end of the garden. There was only one person, I thought, who would be ringing him while we were on holiday. I moved my chair so that I could see him better. He leaned against a broad sycamore trunk, his shoulders sagging. Elva had mastered *Three Blind Mice* and had progressed to *Waltzing Matilda,* which she was playing slowly but tunefully, breathing evenly as Nathan had instructed. Butterflies flitted through the buddleia behind her, weaving between the drooping purple flowers. Dishes clattered in the kitchen as James prepared dinner. He was overseeing Matt and Jess while they made shortbread. He started to sing along to the music . . . 'and he sang as he watched and he waited till his billy boiled' . . . Elva glanced up, smiling.

Nathan snapped his phone shut and walked quickly up the garden to me. He shook his head, his mouth pulled down.

'I need to talk to you,' he said. 'Carry on, Elva, you're doing well.'

I followed him around the side of the house to the front garden. Connie was down on the beach, lying under a lime green parasol, a book held up in one hand. She could never get enough of the sun.

'Veronica?' I asked.

'Yes. Veronica on the warpath. She knows that Elva's here with us and she's not happy.'

'How does she know?'

He cracked his fingers together, an anxious percussion. 'She rang Cedar End.'

'What?'

'She rang the home. Obviously, she had her suspicions. Maybe Matt said something, I don't know. Someone confirmed that Elva was away with you.'

'I don't believe this. What right has she got to ring my workplace?'

'None, but the fact is, she did and she's livid. Says that I've ignored her wishes, trampled on her feelings. She's demanding that you take Elva back to London now or she's going to come and fetch Matt.'

I looked at him, squinting through the sun. He had an air of defeat.

'She's in Richmond at her mother's, May. She can be down here in a matter of hours. She's serious about this.'

I walked to the battered gate and ran my hand along its rough post. The sun and sky looked merciless in the haze.

'It's like being spied on by secret police, or having your neighbours report you. Our life doesn't seem to be ours anymore.' I turned, resting against the gate, needing its solid bulk at my back. 'You're sure she'd actually do that, come and take Matt?'

'Believe me, she will. I could try to stop her but it wouldn't be pleasant.'

'Sounds like we haven't got much choice then,' I said.

'I agree. We need to sort this out but there's no point in taking a stand here. It would only mean major upset for Matt. We'd be going home in three days anyway.'

'It's going to mean major upset for Elva.'

He held his hands out. 'I know, I know. But Matt's my son, I have to put him first.'

'*Your* son. I thought he was ours.'

He sighed. 'Don't, May. It was just a figure of speech. You must see my point.'

'Yes, I see it. I'll tell Elva, then.' I stared at him. 'What am I going to say? I can't tell her the truth – that she has to be removed because she's a possible unsavoury influence.'

We walked out on to the dusty road, discussing what I should tell Elva. The heat from the tarmac drilled through my thin flip-flops. In the end we agreed that I'd say that I had to return to work, to help out, and that I wasn't allowed to leave Elva, because the council was responsible for her. This meant explaining our problem to Lucy, but it was the best solution we could come up with there, under the burning sun, with the careful, steady notes of the saxophone sounding distantly.

I took Elva aside before dinner and explained our lie to her, while Nathan told Connie and James the truth. I poured myself another gin to take up to the bathroom, where she was having a wash. She was obedient to her mother's instructions, always soaping her hands and face before a meal and combing her hair. When I knocked and pushed open the door she was holding a wet flannel in one hand and wielding Nathan's shaving brush in the other. She had worked a lather up around her chin and top lip and was standing on tiptoe to see in the mirror, humming *Waltzing Matilda*.

'I look like the grandfather in Heidi,' she said, delighted with her face.

'Oh,' I said in mock surprise, 'it's Elva! I thought it was another person entirely.' I propped myself on the edge of the bath.

'Does Nathan have to shave every day?' she asked, pushing her lips out.

'Yes. Sometimes he'll shave twice, especially if he's going out in the evening.'

'Doreen used to shave her legs but now she gets them waxed, at Neat and Trim on the Broadway. She says it's downright blue murder but worth it.'

'The things you know,' I said.

She pushed her lips out again. 'I'm practising my embrasure. That's the shape you have to make with your lips when you're playing the sax. Winton Marsalis has a great embrasure.'

There was a stone in my chest. I took a draught of gin and launched into my explanation of our return to London.

'But I'll miss my sax lessons,' Elva said, her voice rising, 'and Nathan said it's important to build up my practise every day.'

'I know, it's really annoying. There's no way round it though, Elva. You can pick up again in London — and I'll talk to Lucy about you attending proper lessons.'

She didn't look convinced. 'It's not fair,' she said, scuffing a foot on the floor. Some fluffs of foam spattered on the tiles.

'No, I know.' I looked down on her bent head. My mouth was dry, parched with gin and the effort of the lie.

'When do we have to go back?'

'In the morning.'

'We're supposed to be going to the aquarium tomorrow. Does that mean I can't go?'

I'd forgotten about the trip. 'I'm sorry,' I said feebly, 'hopefully we can go another time.' A lie to a child must be the worst lie of all, I was thinking.

* * *

Elva didn't eat much of James's cod parcels with peas. It didn't help that Jess and Matt were chatting about the trip to the aquarium and the strange fish they were going to see. Matt was in high spirits, saying that he'd been to an aquarium in Paris with Maman and Michel and he'd seen fish that glowed in the dark.

'Now I'll have been to two aquariums,' he crowed, clapping his hands and spraying peas around. Jess warned him that if he was a bad boy, she'd feed him to the piranhas and Connie told her mildly to behave herself.

The adults were quiet, busying themselves with passing portions. Connie was tight lipped. In the kitchen, as I cut bread, James had put a hand on my arm, saying:

'She's such a bitch, we have to get our heads around this and put a stop to her.'

I couldn't reply, I was sick of myself at that moment. Elva shook her head to ice-cream and slipped away from the table while we were scooping up dessert. Nathan had phoned Veronica back and was looking like a man reprieved from the firing squad. Matt sat on his lap, feasting on strawberry ice-cream and he stretched his hand over mine, squeezing my fingers.

'Thank you,' he mouthed.

While the others cleared away I went to find Elva. I expected her to be upstairs with her jigsaw but the room was empty. She wasn't in the front garden. I peered into the tent. It was dense with the day's heat and held only some bread crusts and damp swimming costumes. Her saxophone was lying on the grass, on top of her open copy of *Reading the Notes, Learning the Music*, with its gaily coloured crotchets and quavers. I brought them inside and searched the other rooms in the house but there was no sign of her. The gin had made me fuzzy headed. I asked Jess if she'd seen Elva and she shrugged a no, flicking her hair. She was absorbed in an encyclopaedia, looking up fish that had a taste for humans.

I walked back out to the front of the house and scanned the horizon. The beach was deserted except for a man in the distance, walking his dog. My heartbeat was too insistent. I crossed the road and stepped down the sloping shingle to the beach, sliding and slipping. Small pebbles skipped into my sandals and scoured the soles of my feet. The sun was directly in my eyes, hanging suspended over the sea. There were a few pale clouds overhead, washed through with rose, like the tie-dyed shirt Jess had worn earlier. It was so quiet, my feet on the shale sounded like an army marching.

I stood, shading my eyes and looked up and down the shoreline. The fort that Jess and Elva had made earlier in the day was being lapped by the incoming tide, its moat brimming with water. There was a low outcrop of rocks further along, hiding some pools where the children liked to play. I walked towards them, moving down on to smooth sand. Far along the shore, the man was throwing a stick for his dog, twirling it through the air, the dog leaping and twisting like a cartoon animal. I licked my lips and swallowed, trying to find some moisture in my mouth.

I crossed the thin stream that split the sand and skirted the edge of the rocks. She was there, near the bigger pool, her back turned to me. She had a yellow plastic spade and was digging fast, tossing sand to one side. My feet were silent on the damp surface and she hadn't heard me approaching. I stood for a moment, calming my heart.

'Elva,' I said quietly. 'I was worried, I couldn't find you.'

She looked over her shoulder quickly. She had a furtive, closed off expression, one I hadn't seen before. She turned away again, hunching her shoulders.

'What are you up to? Building another fort?' I moved closer.

Go away,' she muttered, 'just go away.'

I stepped beside her and looked down. She had dug a deep hole. In the bottom I could see scraps of green canvas and small cars and lorries, a jumble of primary colours.

'That's Matt's bag, isn't it?' I said stupidly.

She threw the spade down and wrapped her arms around her knees, burying her face on them. I reached into the hole and picked out canvas. The bag had been rent into tiny ragged pieces.

I touched Elva's head and she flinched away. I sat beside her, holding the shred of bag, Matt's pride and joy. The dog yelped excitedly, its bark growing fainter. I can retrieve the toys at least, I thought, but I didn't reach for them immediately. I sat, looking at the flushed, shepherd's delight sky while Elva rocked backwards and forwards, lost in her own consoling trance.

The rose sky darkened to mauve. A fishing boat glided out along the coast, its lights dancing like fireflies. I touched Elva's shoulder.

'Look,' I said, 'it's like a painted ship on a painted ocean. Remember the poem?'

She nodded and looked up. 'James says they catch mackerel,' she said nasally. She caught the hem of my skirt. 'Don't tell anyone, please don't tell,' she said. 'They won't want me to come again if they know. They'll say I'm bad and I'm not. I've never done anything like that before.'

I sighed. I could imagine the meal Jess would make of it. And Veronica: if she got to hear of it, it would be more evidence on the charge sheet against Elva. In the end, it was only a bag and some toys, I reasoned. The loss of a bag was as nothing compared to what Elva had suffered.

'That was a nasty thing to do,' I said. 'Matt hasn't done you any harm.'

'I know. I'm really sorry.'

I picked at the shred of canvas. 'I was going to take the toys back,' I said, 'but if I do that, Matt will want to know where the bag is. I think it's best if we just leave everything there and fill the hole in.'

'What will Matt do?'

'He'll be very upset when he can't find his bag. I think you should get him another one with your pocket money, and some cars and vans to replace those.'

'All right.'

'Come on, then. Let's fill this in.'

We heaped the sand back, packing it down, levelling the top, a pair of conspirators burying the evidence. I was going to have to lie to Matt and Nathan, to everyone. My damp hands felt weighted with falsehood.

* * *

Our house was close and airless when I unlocked the door. I picked up the post. There was a large padded envelope for Matt with Veronica's writing on the label. She had stuck Snoopy stickers around his name. I placed it on the hallstand, with the bills. I had a postcard from Cormac. On the front was a picture of a stern Old Testament god with the caption, 'Jesus Is Coming — Look Busy!' I read the card as I wandered through the house, opening windows.

> *Hiya babes, how's it going over the water? I've just come back from Corfu where I met a fascinating Mexican. Ay Caramba! Need a rest now. Hope you're not overheating; the map of the UK is bright orange on the forecast. There's a new bar in Dawson Street you'd love — cocktails to die for including gimlets and the National Gallery have got Picasso, the old goat. Say hallo to Nat and Mattie boy for me.*

PS Your grandmammy would burst a blood vessel if she saw the picture.

I stood under a cool shower, letting the water cascade. I thought back to my flat in Dublin, my calm space with my books and music, my routines of work and gym, films, drinks and theatre visits. I imagined being able to pick up the phone and arranging to meet Cormac later in Dawson Street for a gimlet, the cocktail I'd read about in The Long Goodbye and always wanted to try. I shocked myself as I turned my face into the needles of water and yearned, for just one day, to have it all back.

Guiltily, I dried myself and then went out into the garden. The neighbours had obviously watered but the tomatoes and lettuce were starting to wilt and weeds had sprung up between the courgettes. Some leaves were browning and crinkling. The sunflowers, sturdy survivors, had grown several glossy inches, their heads proud. Everything else looked neglected and careworn. I fetched the hose and gave all the plants a long drink, weeding as each row took its fill of water.

When I was satisfied that I had made amends for the neglect, I cleaned through the house as a kind of expiation for my earlier treacherous thoughts, sweating out my guilt. It was still only two in the afternoon when I'd finished. I showered again and sat in the garden for a while, picking at a sandwich and eating a handful of peas from the pods. It seemed a long three days until Saturday, when I was going to drive back to Norfolk to pick up Nathan and Matt. I felt the sudden absence of company, the heaviness of my own thoughts.

I rang Lucy, who'd been out when I arrived back at Cedar End with Elva. She sounded harassed, as usual, and listened to my explanation of the early return without comment. I sensed that she wasn't much interested in my domestic problems. She sounded more alert when she grasped that I was staying in London until the weekend. Quickly, she asked if I wanted to come back to work as the place was short-staffed and there was one child with a broken leg and another who needed to be accompanied to the police station for interview about a burglary. I agreed, glad to have something to do. She added, drily, that maybe when I came in I could persuade Elva that it wasn't necessary to practise the saxophone for *hours* at a time.

I picked some radishes and peas for Elva, and measured the sunflowers and her courgettes carefully so that I could give her an exact progress report.

* * *

Doreen had sliced a finger open with the carving knife and was sporting a large blue plaster. I helped her with supper, mixing egg mayonnaise for sandwiches.

'Elva's a bit quiet,' she observed, throwing salad leaves into a wooden bowl with her good hand. 'Have a nice time, did you?'

I knew that she was wondering about our early return. 'Very nice, Doreen. Very restful.'

'Crowded, was it?'

'No, surprisingly peaceful, considering the bank holiday's approaching.'

'I've only been that way once, to Hunstanton. Had my fortune told by a gypsy. One of those coach trips, it was. I took the kids. They got sick after eating dodgy steak pies.'

'We ate fish mainly.'

'How's hubby?'

'Fine. Working on his tan.'

'So, a good time had by all.'

'Mmm.'

'That why you're mashing those poor old eggs into a pulp, then?'

'Sorry?'

'They'll be drinking them as egg nog at this rate. You can't fool me, ducks. You and Elva have both got faces like wet weeks.'

I laughed. 'Doreen, you're always a tonic, do you know that?'

So I told her, as I chopped and sliced and spread margarine on bread, sprinkling cress eiderdowns on the egg beds. The monotony of making the platters of sandwiches was soothing. Doreen lit a cigarette, blowing the smoke out the back door, keeping an eye on the corridor in case Lucy might surface.

'Ouch,' she said. 'Sounds like Veronica's got a bad case of cuckoo in the nest. What's her hubby like?'

'I don't know, I've never met him. Neither has Nathan.'

She flicked ash on the back step, formed a smoke ring and poked her finger through it as it floated upwards in the still air.

'There's more to it all than meets the eye, that's for sure. My mum took our cousin in when his parents were killed. My dad and my eldest brother never liked him. There was nothing wrong with him, he was a nice boy. They just couldn't bear him being there, another male on their turf. My mum could never understand it. Of course, it's all psychology these days. We'd have been going to family therapy and seeing shrinks, like some of these kids here.'

'I don't think I'd fancy family therapy with Veronica.' I traced cress around the edges of the plates, knowing that Elva would appreciate the extra touch.

Doreen flapped the collar of her blouse. 'I think it's getting hotter, if that's possible. They reckon the bank holiday's going to be in the 90s.' She came over and looked at the plates of sandwiches. 'Very nice, I'm sure, like tea at the Ritz. You know, ducks, maybe you should just keep the looking after Elva to work. She's all right here, it's not the best place in the world but she's fed and watered and safe. I'd make my own family number one, if I were you.'

'I can't just cut off her visits to us abruptly. Think of what she's been through; it would be an awful, sudden rejection.'

Doreen bent across the table, scooping up crumbs with her broad hand. 'I'm sure you'll do whatever's best,' she said lightly. 'I'll tell you something for nothing, though.'

'What?'

'If I have to listen to *Waltzing Matilda* once again today, I'll go and drown myself in the bleedin' billabong.'

'I'll ask her to give it a rest, or play something else. She's started on *Smoke Gets in Your Eyes*. That would make a change.'

'Let's hope these foster parents they've found are musical.'

'They've found foster parents for Elva?'

'Didn't you know? I thought that's what Lucy was talking to you about in the office. Some people in Essex somewhere. What's his name — that Gary popped in with the news. He's taking her to meet them in a couple of weeks, see if they're "compatible" as he calls it. Right, best put the kettle on.'

I listened to the whoosh of the tap, the rush of water into the huge kettle like rain on a tin roof. My ribs were trapping my breath. Doreen started to sing as she banged the kettle on to the gas, *'you must realize, when your heart's on fire, smoke gets in your eyes.'*

* * *

While the sandwiches were being eaten I rang Nathan. He told me what I already knew, that Matt's bag was missing and nowhere to be found. They'd been looking for it before the trip to the aquarium, so the outing had been miserable and Matt inconsolable. I commiserated, pacing the hallway. I wished that I'd gone straight back to the cottage the night before and told Nathan what had happened, instead of being paralysed by Elva's shame. Now it was too late.

He said that he was sorry that things had gone wrong, I must be fed up and poor old Elva had had a rotten deal. He sounded needy, his voice thin. I asked him to tell Matt that the sunflowers had grown and were still neck and neck and to say to him that I'd had two of his peppery radishes in my sandwich for lunch. I explained that I was at work and had better get back to the children. I mentioned the foster parents and he responded eagerly, that was good, wasn't it, he said, that somewhere with a bit more stability had been found, a proper family. Yes, I agreed, a proper family. I told him I loved him and tucked my phone away. Doreen was telling someone off for dropping crusts. I knew that I would always now associate the gassy smell of eggs with deceit.

CHAPTER 12

Matt was fast asleep. His new bag, a denim replica of the one Elva had destroyed, was at the foot of his bed. Nathan and I were lying on the sofa with the lights off. I had crept into his arms, enfolded him with my body as if he was a lifebelt.

'You feel like home,' I told him.

He patted my shoulder. 'I know, I know.'

He was with me and yet he was distracted, preoccupied with the meeting he was going to have with Veronica. I felt child-like, trying to gain his attention. He nudged a cushion on the floor and nestled back against me, yawning.

'Hope I sleep better tonight,' he said. 'I had a strange dream last night, woke up in a sweat.'

'Yes?'

'I dreamed that Veronica was having me assessed as a fit father and I was waiting for someone official to come and inspect me. I was in a remote house, in a big, dilapidated kitchen. The house started sliding and I realized that its foundations were crumbling. Then I saw that one of the cupboards was full of rotting, stinking meat. Just as I started to clean it out in a sweaty panic the doorbell rang. I woke up then, thank goodness.'

I held his hand. 'I don't think we need Freud to explain that one to us.'

'I found myself looking in the cupboards when I got up this morning.' He laughed. 'I'm a daft sod. Hey, it was so sweet of Elva to buy Matt a bag, and the little cars. When is she meeting the foster parents?'

'Week after next. They're called Kevin and Betty Blake and they have three kids of their own, a boy and two girls. They live in Hornchurch. She's a part-time dental receptionist and he's a manager in a plastics firm.'

'So it's likely that she might be moving there soon.'

'It's possible, as long as the introduction goes OK.'

'It would resolve our major problem with Veronica. That would be quite a relief, a stroke of luck.'

'It would, yes. I hope it's a stroke of luck for Elva, too.' Kevin and Betty: they sounded sensible. I'd pictured them, living in a well-ordered house with a garage and bed linen that matched the towels. Lucy had told Elva of the visit and produced a photograph of the Blakes having a picnic. The first thing that struck me when I saw it was that they were a small family; Betty looked no more than five feet and Kevin only a few inches taller. Their children were shining-skinned, diminutive and bright eyed. The girls wore teeth braces. Their picnic looked well organized, with an array of plastic tubs and a proper gingham tablecloth spread on the grass. Elva had glanced at the photograph, hands held behind her back and said nothing, asked no questions. Then she muttered that she had to go and finish practising her scales and ran to her room. I asked Lucy if the Blakes were musical and she said she didn't know, that finding any foster parents at all was a miracle so it was no good having a specific shopping list. Then she had sighed, said not to worry, this was the hardest bit, Elva would be all right once she'd visited and got the lie of the land. She turned her attention to a missing milk invoice.

It seemed to me that it was Elva who was the miracle; a child who had suffered without any real complaint. I tried to imagine what it would be like to live with foster parents, to experience the disintegration of the homeland you knew and step into a foreign country with a language and customs you'd never heard of. When I voiced this to Doreen she said, 'Trouble with you is you've got too much imagination; some things are best left be.'

'Tell me what you know,' Nathan broke into my thoughts, kissing my forehead.

I pressed my face against his chest. 'I know that if I don't nip out and buy some bread, there'll be nothing for breakfast in the morning. Then Veronica might accuse us of starving Matt, as well as our other sins.'

He pulled back, pressing his hand against my shoulder. 'Don't say things like that, not even as a joke.'

'It wasn't a joke. Who knows what she'll think of next?'

There was silence, then Nathan abruptly swung his legs off the sofa, knocking me aside, and went upstairs. The space he had left held an air of desolation. I smelled the marijuana after a minute, as I knew I would. I threw my dress over my head and followed him. He was cleaning the mouthpiece of his saxophone, the joint smoking on an ashtray.

I brushed my hair, counting twenty strokes. The crackle of static exploded in my head.

'If your joint was a person, what kind of person would it be?' I asked.

He picked it up and pulled deeply on it, considering. 'A loyal, reliable friend. Someone who was always there when I needed them.'

'Do I not fill that bill?'

He smiled at me, pouring more cleaning oil on a rag, but his eyes were fretted with worry. 'You do, May. But this is a friend who asks no questions, makes no demands, a friend who just *is*.'

'Lucky for you then,' I said, 'to have such a friend.' I placed my brush down with quiet fury.

* * *

The bank holiday Saturday dawned with a fierce heat. I listened to the eight o'clock weather and road reports on the radio as Matt and Nathan filled the paddling pool . . . *Traffic already building on the M40 and there are ten mile tailbacks on the M25, anti-clockwise at Junction three* . . . Matt swung off Nathan's leg, yelping with delight whenever his father snaked the hose his way to spray him. I sipped a second cup of coffee and tidied the kitchen, stacking Matt's paintings on a shelf. There was one he had chosen to give to *Maman* later, a picture of a tall house with a red roof and a face inside the top window. It was Veronica's flat in Paris, he explained, with *Maman* looking out of the window. She liked to do that in the evenings and watch people making their way home. She always looked out for him when Papa Michel took him to the park and she waved as soon as he turned the corner.

We were seeing Veronica later in the day, at Connie's. It was James who had suggested that their place would be a good venue rather than our own house or somewhere public. The plan was that Nathan and Veronica could do their talking while we amused the children in the garden, then Connie was going to provide an *alfresco* tea so that we could all sit down and 'be civilized', as she put it. We were hoping that given the news of Elva's foster placement, the meeting could be brief and friendly.

I sighed and checked myself. I had been hearing sighs for the past few days, little exhalations of sound escaping, it seemed that my bones were groaning and creaking, my skeleton unsettled, like the whispering from floorboards in an old house. Nathan was coming through the back door. His face had its closed off, tight look. I stretched my mouth into a greeting.

'Shall we take some beans and salad stuff round to Connie's? We've loads of lettuce.'

'Good idea.' He whistled and looked at the calendar, flipping a page and checking his timetabled trip in the first week of September.

'Is there anything I can do or say to make you feel better?' I asked.

He smiled fleetingly. 'No, I'm fine, really.' He beat out a little percussion with his index fingers on the bread bin. 'You OK?'

'Fine, I'm fine too,' I lied.

* * *

Veronica arrived at 4 p.m. precisely, by taxi. I had gone into the living-room to fetch a book and I looked out from behind the curtain as she paid the driver and came up the steps. She was wearing a smart stone-coloured, sleeveless dress with gold neck chain and bracelet. Her dark glasses were pushed up on to her hair. She rang the bell and Nathan answered, saying good afternoon in a formal voice.

Matt scooted along the hallway, yelling, 'Maman, Maman! I painted a picture of you!' He and Jess had been in the dressing up box. He was sporting a green and gold satin waistcoat several sizes too large for him and had three pink feathers in his hair.

'Did you, darling? That's wonderful, where is it? Goodness, what are you dressed as?'

'Don't know, I just am, just am!' he said, cackling.

I felt like the nameless heroine in *Rebecca*, skulking in the library when the posh relatives come calling. I grasped the book and cleared my throat loudly as I went into the hallway.

'Hallo, Veronica.'

She nodded, fixing her eyes on a point over my left shoulder. 'Hallo.'

'Come and see my picture, it's in the kitchen,' Matt demanded.

We all trooped to the kitchen. It was scented with the strawberry tartlets that Connie was making for tea. Veronica stopped just inside the doorway and greeted Connie, who was whisking cream. Connie stepped forward, clutching her bowl and kissed her cheek. Veronica accepted the kiss, moving back quickly. She carried herself rigidly, crackling with tension.

'Look,' Matt said, proffering the painting, 'it's you at the window, in Paris.'

'Oh, it's wonderful,' Veronica said, 'there I am, looking out for my bonny boy! Aren't you clever?'

Matt beamed, skipping up and down on the spot, feathers waving. 'And look!' he said, 'these are my radishes, May showed me how to grow them.' He grasped several of the purple pink bulbs from the table, earth still dusting their roots, and shoved them into Veronica's hand.

Veronica smiled politely.

'Try one,' Matt urged, 'they're crunchy and like pepper inside.'

'I'd need to wash it first, darling,' Veronica told him. 'Let me look at this lovely picture for now.'

Connie resumed whisking cream and Nathan and I looked on while Veronica examined the painting closely. In the background, Jess was twisting a sari-type garment she'd draped herself with and twanging on a Jew's harp that she'd found in the Oxfam shop at the bottom of the road. It was a strange tableau, lit by the glancing sun; the children exotically garbed, the adults all wearing shorts and creased T-shirts and glistening with suntan cream. Veronica stood in her smart town clothes and jewellery, a cool, sophisticated figure amongst the crumpled garden worshippers. She looked like a person in authority who had come to check out the ne'er-do-wells. I thought of Nathan's dream and glanced at Connie's cupboards; they had grubby paw marks on the doors and one had a broken hinge that had to be banged before it would close properly. Nathan offered coffee and Veronica said black please, no sugar. She smoothed Matt's hair back from his brow, her bracelet clinking softly. Her nails were painted with clear varnish. Nathan placed the coffees on a tray and told Veronica that they could talk in Connie's workroom upstairs, where it would be quiet and shady. He had put a fan up there earlier, saying that anything that kept the heat out of the situation had to be good. Connie ran her finger along the whisk and licked off the excess cream. Then she placed the bowl in the fridge and said in a careful, conversational tone to Matt and Jess that James was convinced that a cat was taking carp from the pond; could they go and count the fish — there should be fourteen.

Jess pulled a knowing face and said, 'Oh OK, if we *must.*'

'I'll come down too,' I said, keen to be busy and out of the house.

I glanced at Nathan; he was already moving towards the stairs with the tray. Veronica walked behind him, holding Matt's painting.

Connie patted my shoulder reassuringly. 'Go on,' she murmured, 'leave them to it, it'll be OK.'

The next time I heard her voice that afternoon, it was raised in the scream that cracked the air and our lives.

* * *

'How can you count fish?' Jess asked. 'It's impossible, because they keep swimming.'

'Well, that's what fish do, that's the point of being a fish in a fish world,' I said.

We had counted over and over and kept coming to different totals. I was deliberately focusing on the pond, resisting any glances towards the open window of Connie's workroom, which was on the first floor at the back of the house.

'It's a fishy business, this,' Jess observed, rearranging the folds of her slippery garment. 'Matt's not helping, that's because he doesn't know how to count.'

'I do know!' Matt protested. He was kneeling by the pond, throwing in blades of grass. 'I think the fish are hiding,' he told me, squinting up. One of his feathers had worked its way around his ear. I stooped and readjusted it with the hairgrips Connie had given him.

'Maybe they're at the bottom, *carping* about us stupid humans.' Jess waved her arms over the smooth surface, throwing a wide shadow.

I laughed and Matt called, 'What does that mean?' He had gone to the edge of the lawn to pick more grass. I was about to explain when he started waving and shouting.

'Elva, it's Elva! Elva's come to tea!' He took off across the lawn, skipping, his bare feet nimble.

I looked up and saw her. She was wearing her tangerine dress and carrying her saxophone. She stood motionless on the patio, knees turned inwards.

'Never mind the carp, that's put the cat amongst the pigeons,' I heard Jess call as I headed after Matt.

I glanced up at the window as I approached the steps leading to the patio. Veronica was standing there, looking out. She was still holding Matt's painting.

'Come and count the carp!' Matt was urging, shaking Elva's arm. 'Jess said I can't count but I can.'

Her eyes were raw and there was a shred of skin hanging from her bottom lip. The saxophone was banging her hip from Matt's agitation of her arm. I took his hand away from her; it was cool from the grass and pond water.

'Shh, Matt, stop yelling.' Then I said, keeping my voice low, 'Elva, what are you doing here? We weren't expecting you.'

She licked her lips. 'I ran away. I don't want to go to Hornchurch. I want to live with you. They can't make me go there, can they?'

'How did you get here?'

'I walked. No one saw me go. I won't get you into trouble, will I?'

Not in the way you mean, I thought. I could hear raised voices above, although I was too startled to make out what was being said.

'The carp keep hiding,' Matt was chatting on. 'They're playing hide-and-seek.'

'Come inside,' I said to Elva, 'you must be thirsty. We'll all have a drink. Here, I'll take your saxophone.'

Connie was standing at the kitchen door, gripping the handle, looking up the stairs. She turned as we came in and pressed a hand across her stomach.

'Elva's run away,' I said. 'She just turned up, she's walked here.'

Connie's lips formed a soundless 0. The saxophone was dragging on my arm. Matt ran to the fridge and reached for a jug of lemonade. As he yanked the door, one of the many magnets clattered to the tiles. Veronica could be heard clearly now, as she came running down the stairs, Nathan behind her.

'. . . I don't believe this, I just don't believe it, I can't trust anything you say to me — bringing that child here today of all days . . .'

She flew into the kitchen and swept Matt up. The jug fell, shards of glass splintering and a waterfall of lemonade swamped my feet. Matt started to cry.

'It's all right, Mattie darling,' Veronica was panting, 'it's all right, Mummy's here.' She pulled his head close under her chin. I put a hand across Elva's shoulder.

'We weren't expecting Elva, this wasn't arranged. She's run away', I said to Nathan.

He shook his head and looked at Veronica. 'My ex-wife was just explaining to me that as she and Michel can't have children, she wants to take my son to live in Paris. She's already been talking to a solicitor, apparently. Elva's going to be used in evidence against me.' His voice trembled. 'Charming, isn't it? Michel can't do the business so I have to smile and lose my son.'

'Nathan, not here,' Connie whispered, gesturing at the children.

'Where, where if not here? You think you're taking my son away, Veronica? You're mistaken!' He stepped forward. 'Give him to me!'

Veronica shook her head, pulling Matt closer. 'I'm going right now,' she said to Nathan, 'with my boy.'

Matt opened his mouth and started howling. Jess ran to her mother, crying, 'she can't take Mattie, can she?'

I looked down at Elva. She was pale, silent, staring at Veronica. 'Can we please stop this and talk more calmly?' I said.

Veronica looked at me directly then, for the first time ever and I saw another person, the veneer stripped by anger. Her cheeks were blotched, her mouth ugly.

'You can keep out of this, it's none of your business. You're the cause of the trouble with that girl, isn't that enough for you?'

'Stop it, Veronica.' Nathan raised his voice over Matt's sobs. 'I am not allowing this. Look what you're doing, for God's sake.'

There was a silence, filled only by Matt's misery and Jess's sniffles.

'Stop crying, Jess, stop it now.' Connie stepped forward. 'We must stop this scene with these children here, right now. Veronica, this is my house and I won't have this.'

Veronica sat on a chair and shushed Matt. He rolled limply against her linen dress. She curled him in against her. She was damp with his sweat and tears.

'I am taking my son now,' she said tightly. 'I am taking him to my mother's. We can talk tomorrow, but not here. I should never have agreed to meet here. Please call me a cab, Nathan.'

Connie looked at him. 'You'd better call the cab,' she said. 'You can't have the child being pulled in two directions.'

Nathan slammed his fist against the wall and went to the phone in the hallway. Connie told Jess and Elva to go into the garden for five minutes while she cleared up the glass. They drifted out through the French windows. I put the kettle on while Connie fetched the dustpan and brush. Veronica sat rocking Matt.

'Shh, shh, Maman's here,' she whispered into his hair. Her mobile phone rang. It was obviously Michel at the other end. '*Attends,*' she said, '*attends un moment.*' She placed Matt on the chair, telling him to wait there, and took her phone into the front room.

'All right, Mattie?' I said.

He looked at me and stuck his thumb in his mouth. He shuddered, pulling his feet up under him. His eyes, Nathan's sea blue eyes, stared back at me. I went to the hallway to where Nathan was on the phone and stood beside him.

'Not easy, getting a cab on a bank holiday,' he said. I touched his arm. He gave me a blank look. 'Get rid of Elva as soon as you can, will you,' he said, 'for God's sake, how long does it take for them to track their own vehicles . . . yes, Richmond, please, as soon as possible . . .'

At that moment there was a dull thump from the road outside and the sound of metal groaning. Then, after a moment of silence came Connie's scream.

CHAPTER 13

I remember some things. I remember looking at Nathan as he dropped the phone and hearing a buzzing, indistinct voice at the other end. I remember running out of the front door into the wall of heat and seeing a jeep turned sideways, Connie on her knees on the road, a man in swimming trunks holding a barbecue skewer laced with sausages shouting into a mobile phone. I remember a woman, the driver of the jeep, saying over and over, 'He just ran out, I didn't stand a chance, he just ran out.' I remember seeing a pink feather by Connie's foot and Elva with her arms folded across her body, standing by the jeep's bumper. And I remember Veronica flying from the house, pushing Connie aside and falling, falling forwards across the body of her son.

I don't remember me. I didn't begin to hear my own thoughts or feel my own skin again until the plane had left Heathrow and the little map on the screen above my head showed our dot in the sky progressing across the Mediterranean. And as I began to think and feel, I longed for oblivion.

* * *

I sat out in the garden at Connie's that night with Jess. Gary had taken Elva to Cedar End. I was dreading a scene but she allowed him to lead her away with no objection and as I watched her drag her saxophone along I knew that I would never see her again. Nathan, Connie and Veronica were at the hospital, at the morgue. The police had gone, their empty teacups on the kitchen table. The strawberry tartlets that Connie had made were wilting on the plate, circled by wasps. Matt's radishes lay beside them and a dish of the beans that were never cooked for dinner. The house was full of emptiness and the fading echo of angry voices.

'We never did count the carp,' Jess said, thumb in mouth.

'No.'

'Will they be back soon?'

'I don't know how long they'll be.'

'Will Elva go to jail?'

'No, of course not. She's a child, it was an accident.'

'She should go to jail. I hate her.' She started crying, thin wails. I put a hand on Jess's arm but she pulled away. I just sat there. I had nothing left to offer.

When I handed in my notice to Lucy, she said in a kind but firm way that she thought it would be best if I didn't see Elva before I left. In fact, she'd spoken to Ms Cartwright and she'd agreed that I didn't need to work my notice period. I understood that I was an embarrassment who might cause awkward questions for her and her manager. I appreciated that she wanted me gone as quickly as possible. It was what I wanted myself.

'How is Elva getting on with the Blakes?' I asked.

'Quite well. Obviously, it's difficult but I think it's promising. Gary is getting some counselling for her so that she has a chance to talk about everything.' Lucy made a steeple of her fingers. 'Have you thought of that yourself, and maybe for your husband, too?'

I nodded, lying. I didn't want her to know that I was staying in a bed and breakfast in Islington, that Nathan didn't want to see me.

'Of course,' she went on quickly, 'if I'd understood how deeply Elva was becoming involved in your family, I'd have stepped in immediately. It was not the best judgement you made, although I understood that you wanted to do your best for her.'

I looked at her, recalling the phone conversation we'd had after my return from Norfolk, when I'd explained about Veronica's objections to Elva. I could have said that no one else at Cedar End had taken much interest in the child; that Lucy herself had hardly been there; that her deputy spent most of her time sorting out her own problems; that I had been left to use my own resources. I said nothing, I was too tired and none of it mattered because the previous evening Nathan's voice had bitten down the phone:

'I don't want to hear you or see you. Nothing you say can make any difference to me.'

'Would you mind if I write Elva a letter, could you make sure she gets it?'

Lucy looked at her desk. 'I don't think that would be a good idea, May. Who would you be doing it for? Best to let things be. I've explained to Elva that this was not her fault; that the adults should have been in charge, that it was a terrible accident.'

I went along the corridor to say goodbye to Doreen. *The adults should have been in charge.* She was opening tins of peaches. When she saw me she shut the kitchen door and made a pot of tea.

'Sit down, gel,' she said, 'take the weight off. You look like you're dragging blocks of concrete.'

I wept a little, then, for the first time, as she got the cups and splashed milk around, lighting a cigarette, but it was as if someone else was crying, someone I was watching.

'You're going, then?' she said, flicking a match on the floor.

'Mm. And I'm going away.'

'Where to?'

'Not sure yet. '

'Oh. What about your husband?'

I gulped tea, not tasting it. 'No, not with him. He's . . . he's not able to talk to me at the moment. He blames me for what happened.'

'But there's no sense in that.'

'No. There's no sense in any of it, it's pointless to look for sense or meaning or whys or wherefores.' *We're somewhere beyond all that, some place never explored before,* I was thinking.

Doreen sighed. 'It's a right old mess, ducks. Little Elva was running away with the boy, was she, because of the mother?'

'Yes. She heard a terrible argument, she was frightened that Matt was going to be taken to France. She was very upset anyway, she'd run away from here that day, she'd turned up saying that she wanted to live with us. Her idea was that she was going to hide somewhere with him until Veronica had gone — the park, probably. Then she thought she'd bring Matt back, so that he'd be safe with Nathan and me. Safe.'

'And that's when he got knocked down?'

'Yes. She was running with him. It all happened so quickly. One minute he was in the kitchen, then Elva had slipped out with him.'

'She's had a rare old time of it. You too.'

'But she's not to blame. I am.'

'You did what you thought was right.'

I looked into the oily tea. It seemed a poor excuse. I put the cup down. 'My grandmother used to say, "The road to hell is paved with good intentions".'

'Funeral all over and done with?'

'Yes, Matt was cremated.'

151

I hadn't gone to his funeral. Connie told me that Nathan didn't want me there. 'Don't take it to heart, please don't,' she'd said as she dropped me off at the small hotel, 'he doesn't know what he's doing or saying. He needs time, his mind is unwell.'

'Well — that's understandable, in the circumstances. Poor kid, he was full of beans. Would have been a right charmer when he grew up, I thought that day he was here.'

She lit another cigarette and blew a smoke ring. We both watched it drift towards the door and dissolve into a thin blue mist.

* * *

In the evenings, in the small hotel room, I thought about the garden. The tomatoes would need tying back and any stray shoots should be clipped off. The last of the beans would be ready for harvesting. But it hardly mattered; the height of the sunflowers, the growing girth of Elva's marrows, the healthy mauve blush on Matt's radishes, these important daily details that had caused so much conjecture and pride were lost to us all. I thought of Nathan's dulled eyes, the hard sobs that I heard from behind a locked bathroom door, the stubble on his chin that he couldn't be bothered to shave off. Slowly, clumsily, he paced through the house without purpose. He sat for hours with his eyes closed or just looking into space. The only time he was roused was when he spat words at me. I suppose I could have tried harder to break the numbing ice around Nathan's heart. I think that deep down, I didn't want to. I felt the burden of guilt and I sought punishment. I needed to exile myself. Perhaps if we had been together longer, we would have been stronger. Exceptional circumstances call for exceptional strength. When I heard his harsh, cutting words I knew the meaning of mad with grief. We were both unhinged, our minds teeming with: if I had only . . . if she hadn't . . . if we had realized . . .

How can love go so wrong? I asked myself in the narrow bed that reminded me of Cedar End. 'I meant no harm,' I whispered. There was no one to answer me.

So I went to the airport, the London streets flashing by, tired and drab with the end of the heat wave. I looked at the departure boards, destinations winking and approached a check-in desk. When a woman said, 'May I help you?' I heard Matt's gurgling giggle the day when Nathan introduced us and made my name into a word game. The flight to Rhodes was in an hour. I booked a ticket.

* * *

I came back to London a month ago. Connie was our intermediary, our dedicated seamstress who patched us together with letters and phone calls. The shape, the pattern we make isn't clear yet, it's too early to say. When I saw Nathan at the airport I felt as if my bones were glass shards beneath my skin. I wanted to fall against him but I kissed his cheek, touched his arm and we talked of the weather and travel delays, the route we would take through London because of road works.

In the car, queuing in traffic, I said, 'I'm still your kith and kin.'

He made no reply but laid a hand on mine momentarily. Then he said, 'Your hair is short.'

'Yes, It was too hot on the islands to keep it long, too uncomfortable.'

'Do you think you might grow it again?'

'I could. Would you like that?'

'I would, yes,' He paused. 'Then you'd be the Spanish lady.'

I have been holding that small nugget of hope in my hand, like a comforter.

* * *

We came here to the cottage a few days ago. Nathan sleeps heavily into the mornings, lulled by anti-depressants and whisky. The pills don't stop him dreaming and shouting in his sleep. He is thinner, as is his hair, the curl gone. The morning after Matt's death, he woke to find half of it on his pillow. His skin is dry and papery. When we make love, tenderly but hesitantly, his body feels tense. We embrace each other carefully, breathing lightly, as if a wrong word or move might shatter our fragile bond. At times I feel that he is arguing with himself as he holds me. For months into my travels, I woke expecting to hear Matt's clattering. In a beach cafe on Crete I tasted cinnamon in my croissant and left my coffee and food untouched.

I've promised Nathan that I will never try to contact Elva or find out about her. I think of her often still, a nagging memory like a tongue seeking out a painful tooth. I wonder if she is still with the Blake family, whether she plays her saxophone and gardens. Maybe she will grow vegetables and flowers when she is an adult, remembering what I showed her about planting and watering. Maybe that is one good thing I passed on to her, as my father did to me. I have a recurring dream that when she is older she will find me and blame me for what happened to her, for abandoning her.

Nathan told me that the garden had gone to seed in the last year and when I saw it I wanted to weep at the confusion of weeds. I haven't touched it. We will be selling the house and the new buyers can tackle it.

It is just half past eight and the sky holds a mist that won't clear today. This is as warm as it will get. I am wearing my swimsuit under my jeans and jumper. I slip them off and step into the restless sea. Goose pimples rush my skin. I swim parallel to the shore, up and down, my teeth chattering, wanting the chill waves to wash me clean and whole. When I am warmed through and tired I dry myself and dress and make my way back to the cottage.

I make breakfast, toast with Connie's greengage jam and tea and take it upstairs. Nathan is just waking, reaching for his first joint of the day. I put the tray down but leave the curtains closed so that the light stays dim. We talk more easily in shaded rooms.

'Been in the briny?' he asks when I bend down to kiss him. He touches my cheek with his hand. His breath smells of whisky and the staleness of the night.

'Yes, it's chilly. Eat something before you light up, please?'

His shoulders tense and I think that he will snap at me but he takes a slice of toast.

'I always liked making you breakfast,' I tell him, 'I always liked the way you stretch and rotate your feet. I'd like to make you breakfast when you're very old.'

He swallows and looks at me. 'Thank you for saying that. I feel very old now, old and grey and full of sleep.'

'You won't always feel that way.'

'No? Maybe.'

I make my voice light. 'We could have a walk this morning,' I say. 'Maybe stop at the greengrocer, get some salad stuff.'

'Fine. Don't forget we've got Connie's tomatoes.'

'I could make soup. Buy some basil and cream.'

'Mmm. Sounds promising. Tea's fine and strong.'

'Good. It's a nice blend, an Assam.'

We sip in silence, crumbling toast, licking the sticky glue of greengage from our fingers. We are close acquaintances; people who once met vividly on shore, then boarded different vessels. I know that he must be struggling with the same insistent thought as me: *can we find it again, can we get us back, is that possible?*

I don't know what we are allowed, whether the grace that favoured us will fall on us again. I don't dare to imagine how these things are measured and how they come about.

I take Nathan's empty cup and place it on the tray. This is how it will be, I think, this will be the measure of our hours for now: we will be kind to each other. We will sit and talk slowly, choosing our words. We will walk in the cool of this September and eat simple meals. In the evening we will light the fire and read together as night comes calling, content to have paced our way through another day.

THE END

Thank you for reading this book. If you enjoyed it please leave feedback on Amazon, and if there is anything we missed or you have a question about then please get in touch. The author and publishing team appreciate your feedback and time reading this book.

Our email is jasper@joffebooks.com

www.joffebooks.com

ALSO BY GRETTA MULROONEY

ARABY
MARBLE HEART
OUT OF THE BLUE
THE LADY VANISHED